THE ELEVENTH TRADE

ALYSSA HOLLINGSWORTH

THE ELEVENTH TRADE

Roaring Brook Press
New York

Library of Congress Control Number: 2018936543

ISBN: 978-1-250-15576-4 (hardcover)
ISBN: 978-1-250-15577-1 (ebook)

Our books may be purchased in bulk for promotional, educational,
or business use. Please contact your local bookseller or the Macmillan
Corporate and Premium Sales Department at (800) 221-7945 ext. 5442
or by e-mail at MacmillanSpecialMarkets@macmillan.com.

First edition, 2018
Book design by Aimee Fleck
Printed in the United States of America by
LSC Communications, Harrisonburg, Virginia

1 3 5 7 9 10 8 6 4 2

To Zarmina, Maliha, Fareed, Rasheed, Hamida,
Hajji Chamin, and Hajji Habibullah.

Remember tea in Kabul? You told me what
you wished other people knew about Afghans.

Thank you.

Also, for the woman in the unmarked
grave on a quiet Tennessee hill.

1

BABA'S FINGERS ARE QUICK ALONG THE REBAB'S STRINGS. He doesn't see me right away, so I hang back, listening to the music, enjoying the glow that seems to fill him when he plays. But then his eyes catch mine, and his smile widens into something just short of a laugh.

"Ah, son of my son, the young scholar!" he calls in Pashto. "And how was the new school?"

"Good." Speaking the language of our people—the Pashtuns—brings me relief after struggling through English all day. I hurry toward the light of Baba's eyes, the sound of his music. For the first time today, it feels like my skin fits. I drop my frayed backpack beside Baba, the Manchester United key chain jingling against the wall. The brick floor probably had color at some point, but it's all covered in grime now. I sit and fold my legs, careful to tuck my feet under my thighs like my mor, my mother, taught me. "Really good, I think."

Baba nods, and his strumming fills the stuffy air with music. The twangy sound bounces around the tight subway tunnel in loud echoes.

A man drops a twenty-dollar bill into the rebab case. I get a glimpse of his neatly trimmed beard and smile. He's gone into the crowd before I can say thanks.

Back in Afghanistan, before the Taliban came, Baba was a famous performer. People would pay thousands of Afghani to hear him play. Here, rush-hour Bostonians leave a wide space around us with a funny looking-not-looking expression on their faces. Some of their steps pound a rhythm to match Baba's song. Others walk out of sync, footfalls clashing against the tempo. My brain keeps wanting to blend the off-beat movement into the music.

"And have you made any friends yet?"

"No." I focus on pressing a wrinkle in my jeans flat. I'm not sure I even looked anyone in the eyes all day. "But I was able to follow the reading exercise in language arts without too much trouble."

Around the bend of the corridor, someone begins singing scales.

"Ah, the opera singer and her stereo have arrived," Baba observes. Once she starts "Ave Maria," we'll have to pack up. It's impossible to compete with an opera singer.

"Isn't it cheating to use a stereo and mic when you're already louder than the whole city?" I ask.

"Don't be disrespectful," Baba chides. "But yes, it is definitely cheating." Baba stops playing and checks the coins in the rebab's case.

Hiding my own grin, I help him scoop the coins into his wallet.

"Want to have a turn, Sami?" Baba asks, passing the rebab to me. The opera singer cranks up her stereo, and the first cheesy violin notes drift down the tunnel. "I will just go wash my hands, and then we can head home."

"They say 'go to the bathroom' here," I remind him, taking the rebab.

"I'll go to the *bathroom*, then." His eyes crinkle. "I have a special dinner planned when we get back, and I want to hear more about your first day at school. Then—if we find the right radio channel—we can listen to that Champions League final before bed."

"All right." I adjust the rebab in my lap, singing one of the Manchester United chants, "Hello! Hello! We are the Busby Boys!"

Baba hums as he wanders off. I flick my fingers over the rebab's three main strings. The mulberry-wood base presses into my chest. One aid worker called it "boat shaped." It's deep enough that I have to wrap my right arm all the way around to reach the strings. The old goatskin covering the sound box still has a cream color at the center, but fades to a blotched brown on the edges and under the place I rest my fingers. Where the skin meets the wooden neck, mother-of-pearl inlays flash white, blue, green, and pink in the dim subway light. The pegbox at the end of the neck is carved in a flower design, with one end chipped from where Baba dropped it in Iran. The tassel—woven by my grandmother in blue and white string with red beads—swings as I adjust the rebab in my lap.

I take a slow, deep breath.

Songs always come to me if I wait still and quiet enough. Sometimes they're songs I've heard Baba perform. But sometimes they're something else—songs that travel a great distance and play through my hands like they aren't mine at all.

Those are the most fun.

I begin to play, and my left hand dances over the rebab's neck. I keep my right wrist loose and easy, strum-flicking. The beat builds in me, and the opera singer's voice and the commuters' footsteps fade. The outside world gets smaller and smaller, until it's just me and the rebab.

But the world inside me expands. Even though my eyes are closed, I see my home. Not the apartment here in Boston, or the slum in Istanbul, or the cramped hostel in Athens, or the back room in Iran. I see my Kandahar house.

It is white stone with a high wall all around. The shattered glass on top of the wall sparkles in the afternoon light, the shards bright blue and sometimes yellow, like broken bits of sky. Pink bougainvillea flowers nod in a rare afternoon breeze. A workman repairing a hole in the roof of our house hums the song I'm playing now.

I play harder, louder, smelling the dust and dry heat and feeling the sun warm my neck.

My plar, my father, reads by the window, his glasses sliding down his nose. My mor jani calls to him. We are all going to be late for the wedding if he doesn't hurry. But I can't hear her, my memory is not sharp enough. Her henna-decorated palms are red when she leans out the door to wave me in. Her mouth moves, but I no longer remember the sound of her voice.

I'm almost there. Every time I play, I can almost hear her.

But I can't quite make the memory clear, and even as the music rises, even as it pulls me in until the notes are sharp, quick pings, I am losing. I am losing the memories.

Was my plar's hair graying, or was it black as tar on

a kite string? Was my mor jani's voice bright, or was it weary? Did the workman smoke, or did he sing?

I squeeze my eyes closed tighter in concentration. I'm losing them—

Something jolts the rebab.

Suddenly my hands are empty.

My eyes fly open. A teenager hurries with the crowd toward the platform. The rebab is in his hand. He snatched it from my lap.

For three long heartbeats, I'm too stunned to move.

Then I scramble to my feet. "Hey!" I wheeze, trying to get enough air to speak. My legs steady, and I start to run. "Hey! Stop!" My voice still comes in a squeaking whisper.

We're both heading toward the opera singer, and her song lifts to a deafening crescendo. I can't even hear myself yell over the volume of her speakers.

A man's elbow almost knocks my eye, and a woman's briefcase blocks me from squeezing past her. Far ahead now, in a sudden shift of the crowd, I spot the teenager's black coat. He must have tucked the rebab inside, because I can't see it anymore.

"Stop!" I shout, my voice cracking with the effort.

No one listens, least of all the thief. I press against arms and legs, but they push back.

"Watch it," snaps a young woman.

"Back off," growls an older man.

A sudden surge pushes me onto the platform. It's packed so tightly I can't spot the thief at all. I slide along the wall and jump up on the edge of a bench where a bunch of college students are sitting. Balanced on one foot, I scour the crowd.

The train arrives. Everyone presses into the already crowded cars.

There! The thief shuffles onto the train and pushes his way toward the center. The rebab is in his right hand.

"*Stop!*" I scream. A few heads turn. I lunge off the bench, but too many people press between me and him. The adults tower above me. I shove my shoulders against their arms, fighting my way forward.

The T train gives two loud beeps. The doors are closing.

I burst free at the platform's edge. The doors slide shut right in front of my nose.

The teenager is only a few feet away. He glances at me, and his eyebrows lift a fraction. He's pimply, the redness bright on his pale skin, and he has gray eyes and shaggy blond hair.

"Stop him!" I bang on the window and wave at the passengers. The train begins to move, slowly at first. I run beside it, down the bumpy danger strip where the adults aren't standing. "Please—please—!"

The people in the train don't hear, or don't care. The speed builds, and I'm falling behind. I'm falling away from the rebab.

Then, with a *swoosh*, the train disappears into the tunnel. I'm standing on the platform, breath heaving, ears ringing.

The rebab is gone.

2

BABA IS ALREADY AT OUR SPOT WHEN I RETURN. HE looks rapidly between the rebab case and the crowd. Searching for me.

Even though I can see he's worried, my feet drag. I keep near the wall to avoid the crush of people on their way to the platform. My chest feels like it's filled with sand.

The opera singer has moved on to "Think of Me," and I resist the urge to kick her stereo as I walk by.

The rebab was the only thing that survived our escape. The only thing left of home. The only way Baba made money.

I've lost it.

Baba sees me, and his shoulders give a big heave. I walk faster. When I was ten, shortly after we arrived in Istanbul, I got lost in the market. All the colors spun and burned in my head, and I ran, ran until my legs shook and my breath rasped—and when I found Baba, we hugged and cried right in the middle of the street. I want to throw my arms around him now, but I can't. I'm twelve and too old for that.

And anyway, this time it's my fault.

"Sami, where were you?" he asks in rapid Pashto, checking my head like he thinks I've injured myself. "Why did you leave? Are you all right?"

I open my mouth, but nothing comes. He seems satisfied that I am in one piece, and his expression changes from worry to confusion.

He glances at my hands and the empty case. "Where is the rebab?"

I lower my gaze. I can't whisper—not with the opera singer's noise—but I struggle to get my voice strong enough. "A teenager snatched it out of my hands. He jumped on the T."

"What?" Baba says, suddenly quiet.

"He stole it and ran away." I stop. Swallow. "The thief's gone. The rebab's gone."

Baba does not speak. He's so silent. I glance at his face. His skin is gray, and his eyes are wide and dark.

I feel so tight I might snap, like one of the rebab's strings. I wish he'd say something. I wish he'd yell. I wish he'd strike me. I wish he'd do anything to stop looking like that.

"It is all right, Sami," he says at last, so soft I read his lips more than hear the words. He pats my head and leaves his hand resting on my hair. "It is all right. We will be all right. Khuday Pak mehriban dey."

God is kind. If that's true, why do I feel like he betrayed us—again? I keep the biting, broken question to myself.

"We can report it to the police," I say. "Maybe they could catch him."

Baba shakes his head absently. I'm not sure if he does not want to report it because he doesn't trust the police— he never has—or because he's too tired.

He does not say any more. Not when we pack up the empty case. Not when we take the T home. Not when we walk down the alley to our apartment. Not when he makes dinner. We spread the dastarkhan—the tablecloth—on the floor and lay out the meal together—chicken kebabs, naan, and watermelon, my favorites. Baba must have planned this special dinner for my first day of school. He produces two Cokes and passes one to me. My stomach shrinks.

His voice is wispy and old when he asks, "So school was good?"

11

"It was fine," I say. "Different, but—fine."

He nods. Just the single question seems to have exhausted him, and he does not ask more. We eat in silence. I can't remember the last time we didn't talk during a meal, and the strangeness creeps into the air around us like smoke. The food tastes flavorless, and the soda hurts my throat. As soon as I am done, I sneak away into our second room—a shared bedroom. The two mattresses lie directly on the floor against opposite walls. I sit on mine and open a math book to study.

It's strange to start a new school in May—I only have about a month until summer. But the aid agency that brought us to America had me take a few tests and recommended that I be placed immediately.

I'm nearly done with my homework when the window in the living room scrapes as Baba wedges it open. The mosque down the street begins the azaan for maghrib prayers. I join Baba, facing toward the qibla, the direction of Mecca. We recite the familiar words together, and I hope God hears my silent plea as we bow on our musty-smelling prayer rugs. *Please.*

Please . . . what? We lost so much when we fled Afghanistan. Sometimes I think the only thing that kept us from breaking was the rebab. It was our heart and our past, but it was also a promise. It was our hope.

But now there is nothing. Only silence. And this void has come from me. I caused Baba pain. The rebab was taken from *my* hands. And how can I undo that? Without our songs, what will be our hope?

Please, please, please, I pray. Please what? I can't find the words to finish the prayer. *Please, please, please,* I continue, trying to trust that the cracks in my chest will show God what my words are missing. *Please.*

When we finish, Baba settles on the toshaks against the wall. They're not really toshaks, though—they're just big pillows. He slides one photograph out of his worn leather wallet. Even though I can't see it from here, I know what it is: a picture of my mor and plar at their first wedding anniversary, both wearing serious expressions, though their eyes smile. The wrinkled photo paper has browned at the corners. An uncle mailed it to us while we were in Istanbul. It's an echo of a song, a faded glimpse of our old life.

I sink down on the toshak beside him. "What will we do, Baba?"

"We thank God for our fortune. Alhamdulillah." He puts an arm around me and rubs my shoulder.

"Should we go to the police?"

"No." His response comes quick and strong. I stiffen. His hand pauses, then continues in the same steady rhythm.

"We do not raise problems. We do not ask for more when we have all we need. Besides, we will have a few months of living stipend from the agency. That will keep this apartment, at least. And I can find a job to take care of the rest. Perhaps the Indian restaurant on the corner needs a dishwasher."

I think of Baba, whose playing used to make weary people dance and broken people laugh, wasting his hands on dirty dishes. As the image lingers in my head, the rest of the prayer springs into my mind so suddenly I almost gasp.

Please help me make it right.

Something in me hardens. I don't say anything, because I know it's crazy even before the idea has fully formed in my head. But I vow it in my heart.

I'll get the rebab back.

3

BUT THE NEXT DAY, I'M STILL NO CLOSER TO A
solution. I know when, where, and how the rebab was
stolen. I know what the guy looked like. But I don't
know why. What does he want with a stolen rebab? I
can't imagine he cares about playing it. The only thing
I can think is that he wants to sell it.

I head into the boys' bathroom at school, still turning the problem over in my head. In Afghanistan, he
probably would have taken it to another town's market.
But there aren't markets like that here—not that I've seen.

Every stall in the bathroom is covered with graffiti,
though the walls of the last two are faded from recent
scrubbing. I slip into the farthest stall, gaze glancing
over the words *Ms. Nolan sucks!* After I've done my business, I hear the bathroom door open, and two boys my
age come in.

I go to the faucet without looking their way. They pay me as much attention as a tile on the wall.

"Pete *really* got it this time," says one boy. His skin is a little darker than mine and his hair about an inch shorter, just a buzz cut. "The pawnshop owner recognized his picture right away."

"I heard it was Jim who actually stole the bracelet, though," the second, shorter boy chimes in. "He just told Pete to sell it, and Pete did without ever realizing it belonged to Ms. Nolan!"

I slowly dry my hands with a paper towel, but my thoughts are racing. Pawnshop? Is that a place where people can sell stolen things?

"Yeah, well, Jim didn't make him do all *this*," the first boy says, laughing. In the mirror, I see him gesture to the graffiti on the stalls.

I exit into the hall and check my printed schedule, just to be sure I know where I'm going. Study session next, which means I'll be expected in the library. I head in that direction, repeating the new word in my head: *Pawnshop. Pawnshop.*

Other kids call greetings to each other or cluster around lockers. Down the hall, some students start shouting. A fight. I keep my head down and duck into the library.

I slide into a chair at an unused computer. It still feels exciting—the musty smell of books and carpet, the ease of internet that actually works. Google loads so fast I hardly have time to open my phone's note app before a list of results about pawnshops fills the monitor.

Turns out, a pawnshop is a place where people can sell stuff for money. According to one article, stolen goods can be sold at a pawnshop—that's one of the risks the owner takes when he makes a purchase. So it seems possible our rebab ended up in a shop like that.

I run a map search and find about forty pawnshops in the Boston area. My heart sinks a little. But it's something, and that's more than I had this morning. I copy down the nearest address onto my phone.

The computer next to mine is taken by someone, but I don't look over, and he doesn't say anything. Out of the corner of my eye, I see him pull up Tetris and begin to play.

Once I finish typing out the addresses of the first ten pawnshops, I stick my phone into my backpack. My Manchester United key chain hangs from the zipper. It's metal painted gold and red. The crest of a crowned lion spins in the middle. Baba bought it for me when the team beat Liverpool last year. And suddenly I realize: The Champions League final was yesterday. Baba and I forgot!

I open a new tab and type in a search. Maybe if Manchester United won, it will help Baba feel better. At the very least, I can read the match news and tell him everything about it tonight.

I open the first article that comes up, and right there in bold font is the headline *Final Faux Pas: Pitiful Penalties Cost United Champions League Glory.*

Barely keeping in a groan, I scan the article. A video plays automatically while I'm scrolling, and I stop reading to watch. It's the penalty kick. Manchester's man lines up the shot, the one that *should* have taken the game. But as he prepares to kick, I can already tell what he's going to do. This player always kicks to the far right—I know it; the goalie knows it. This time is no different. The goalie catches the ball easily, and just like that, they've lost.

This time I really do groan, rubbing a hand over my face in frustration. I mutter, "He should have at least *tried* to fake the keeper."

"Yeah," says the kid next to me. "That was terrible."

I jump. I hadn't realized the kid was watching my screen. His hair is spiked with gel, and he's wearing a T-shirt with three yellow triangles on it. Even now, he's watching while the video plays over again.

He adds, "I would've done a Panenka, definitely. That could have carried the game."

A Panenka is a pretty daring move—where the player tricks the goalie into moving right or left, then shoots the ball down the middle. As I look again at the video, I see how it would have worked. "You're right. See?" I point to a moment when the goalie veers a fraction to the side. "He would have gone right and missed it."

The kid looks impressed. "Hey, aren't we in language arts together?"

Now that he says it, I realize he does kind of seem familiar. I nod.

"Cool. Have you ever played—"

Before he can finish, someone drops into the chair on the other side of him, elbowing him. In an undertone, the guy whispers, "Hey, Dan, what are you doing after practice?"

While the first kid—Dan—is distracted, I grab my backpack, sign off of the computer, and slip out of the library. Dan doesn't even notice.

It was kind of nice to talk to someone about goal-kicking strategies, but I'm more comfortable on my own. Besides, I have something better to do—I have a list of pawnshops.

Which means I have a plan.

4

FOR THE NEXT WEEK, I USE MY TIME AFTER SCHOOL
to search for the rebab while Baba works. He started his
new job as a dishwasher the day after the rebab was stolen. In the same time, I've visited six of the forty pawnshops and haven't found anything. My plan is starting
to feel like a long shot, but it's my only lead. Today I'll
leave from Roxbury to go to Reed Jewelers and Pawnbro-
kers by the Ruggles T stop. I check that my train pass—
my CharlieCard—is still in my pocket, and I head across
the parking lot toward the street. Students gather in
small groups near the basketball court and the bus
pickup.

A group of seventh graders are kicking a ball in an
informal game on the playground. They've put two soda
cans on either side to mark the goals. The tallest kid
maneuvers easily around his opponents—even in the

short time it takes me to walk past, I see him score point after point. The kid from my language arts class—Dan—is playing defense, but he isn't holding up well.

I continue across the parking lot, and my stomach growls. Yesterday was the first day of Ramadan. The full fast is not required at my age, but in Kandahar I would have started learning to fast back when I was ten. Baba and I were exempt during our travel, so it feels important to participate this time. Plus I hope that if I join Baba in the tradition, bringing a bit of home into our lives here, he'll feel the sting of losing the rebab a little less.

I haven't eaten or had a drink since before dawn, and I won't until sunset. It is only 3:10 now, so breaking the fast—iftar—is still five hours away.

Today's the hardest, I tell myself. *It will be easier tomorrow.*

"Get it!" someone shouts. "Catch it before it goes in the street!"

I turn and see my classmates racing after their runaway ball. It's skidding toward me, a few feet to my right. I jog toward it, stop the ball with my foot, and kick it over the head of the tall guy on offense.

With a bounce, it lands at the feet of an astounded-looking Dan. The tall one shoots me a dirty look as he pivots away, and all the defenders follow him with their eyes. But Dan's still looking at me, so I gesture to the

21

goal. Dan catches on, turns, and shoots the ball across the playground into the unguarded opening. It bangs against the chain-link fence.

"Yeah!" Dan yells, fist-pumping the air.

"Doesn't count!" the tall one shouts over the celebrating team. "The ball was out!"

I grin to myself and keep walking. But I've barely gone three steps when someone calls my name. I look around, surprised anyone even knows who I am.

"Hey, Sami!"

It's Dan. I hesitate, unable to decide if I should wait or run. Several of the other kids watch as Dan jogs toward me, and my chest tightens. All the people looking at me makes my hands sweat.

I turn away, but Dan has almost reached me. "Hey, wait up, Sami!" he calls. "Hold on!" And now he's tapping my shoulder. I have no choice but to look at him.

The tall one cups his hands around his mouth. "You just going to leave the game, Dan? We haven't finished!"

"I've got to go anyway!" Dan waves the guy off. "It's just a pickup game," he says to me by way of explanation. "My real team plays at the gym. Anyway. That was *awesome*! Perfect pass!"

His enthusiasm is overwhelming and *very* loud. I don't know how to respond, so I just stand there silently.

He doesn't even take a breath. "You really like soccer?" he asks.

Football, my brain translates.

"Oh," I say. "Yeah, I guess."

"You any good?"

"Yeah," I say again, though it's been a while since I played. "I guess."

"I'm on a team at this after-school place. They've got an indoor gym and we practice all year. We just lost a player, so I'm looking to add a new offense guy. You play offense? Forward, maybe?"

I blink. He's talking extremely fast, but I think he's asking me to join his football—soccer—team. I'm not here to play soccer, though. I just want to keep my head down. Study hard. Find the rebab. Minding your own business is the way to survive when you're always on the move.

Except Baba and I aren't on the move anymore.

"Um, maybe." I edge away from him. "But I have to go . . . somewhere . . . now. Roxbury Crossing T stop."

"You walking?" he asks, following me. "The gym's this way. I'll show you."

I don't want to see the gym. I just want to find the rebab. But I can't think of a good excuse—one that won't make him more curious—and now Dan is staring at me weirdly.

"Okay," I say, trying to sound calm. "Okay, yeah, lead the way."

"Wicked." He gives me two thumbs up and starts off. He strolls down the sidewalk with his head high and his back slouched. I try to copy him as I follow. But he walks like the streets are his, and I walk like, well, like they're his, too.

"So, where're you from, Sami?"

"Afghanistan," I say, and wait for him to tell me what he thinks of my country. Every American has opinions about Afghanistan.

"For real? Bet you were glad to get out. My dad did a tour there. He said it was—" Dan glances at me and grins. "Well, he said it wasn't great."

I think about the time before everything changed, when we had family dinners with a kerosene lantern during power outages, and Baba plucked the rebab's strings whisper quiet, in case our neighbors were Taliban sympathizers. It was under the Taliban that music became illegal, and even the arrival of foreign forces didn't always keep the Taliban from attacking people who broke their rules. It was a little exciting, back then. Exciting to feel like our family was a secret, our songs were a secret.

But that was before the wedding.

I want to tell Dan his dad is wrong, and Afghanistan

has beautiful mountains and blue skies and more stars than you can see anywhere on this side of the world. But *that* Afghanistan—the one where you do not lose your family a little every day, where you do not live in fear of turning the Taliban's head—does not really exist outside of my heart. I didn't know how to explain it to people in Iran or Greece or Turkey, and I don't know how to explain it to Dan.

It'd be easier if I had the rebab. Then I could play, and he would hear.

"Your dad is a soldier, then?" I ask instead.

"Yep. In the army." Dan cups his mouth and shouts at some pigeons, "HOOAH!"

The pigeons scatter, and Dan laughs. I glance around to see if anyone has noticed us, but none of the walkers seem to care.

"There's the gym." Dan points to a gray building. "You want to go in?"

It's fenced with high chain-link and razor wire spun across the top. I touch the scar on my arm, then check my phone. Three fifteen. The pawnshop doesn't close until five, but I say anyway, "Oh, I can't. I have to go. Sorry."

"Wow, *that's* your phone?" Dan exclaims, tapping my screen. "Looks like my first one, and I got that *years* ago. Do you have any cool apps?"

I glance from him to the phone. It sends and receives texts and takes notes, and its map works when I find free Wi-Fi or when we pay extra for data, like we did during our journey. That was all we needed it to do. "No?"

Dan takes out his phone. It's thinner than a pencil and bright green, with an expensive shine to it. I inch back, as if by looking I might accidentally break it.

"So," Dan says, scrolling through screens and then showing me his calendar. The only appointments on it are labeled *SOCCER!!* "Want to come tomorrow after school?"

"Maybe. But I have to go now."

"Where are you going, anyway?" he asks.

I hesitate, but nothing comes into my head except the truth. Before I can stop myself, I blurt out, "Someone stole my baba's instrument. I'm searching for it in pawnshops." I immediately wish I could take the words back. Dan doesn't need to know something so personal about me.

"Nah, I don't think you'll find it there." Dan glances down at his phone and starts typing. "What sort of instrument?"

A little annoyed that he's texting, I say simply, "A rebab."

"Like the vegetable?"

"No . . . ? It's an Afghan instrument. A lute, sort of."

"Umm . . . Okay, spell it." While I do, Dan taps and swipes. "This same thing happened to Father Steve—he's a priest at my church. His guitar got stolen. Turned up on eBay. And . . ." He shows the screen to me. "Is that yours?"

I gape. A picture of a rebab is on the listing. He wasn't texting—he was searching. Reaching tentatively for the phone, I ask, "Can I see?"

Dan hands me the phone. I try to hold it carefully as I tap through the pictures. They're sharp and clear, with a clean white background, taken with a good camera. But I know it's Baba's rebab—it has a blue, white, and red tassel and star-shaped designs along the side. I can hardly believe Dan found it so quickly—I've been searching for a week!

"That's ours." I raise my head and look him in the eyes for the first time. "How do I get it?"

"Let me see." Dan takes the phone back and types. "The lister owns a shop in Cambridge, apparently. The address is on his profile. Here, I can text it to you."

I give him my number, and a few seconds later the message dings on my phone. My hand over my heart, I bow my head out of habit. "Thank you!"

"No prob." Dan grins and copies me, hand over his heart.

I hesitate, unsure if he's mocking me. But before

I can decide, he's running into the gym's courtyard, calling "See you tomorrow" over his shoulder.

I have no thoughts about tomorrow—the rebab is just across the Charles River right now! I run down the sidewalk, jumping the spring weeds in the cracks.

The Roxbury Crossing T stop is just around the corner. I need to get to the music shop and return home before Baba leaves work, or else he'll know I'm up to something. And my plan is so new, I can't share it with anyone yet.

I swipe my CharlieCard at the turnstile, say a prayer, and wait for the train.

The address takes me to Creature Guitar, a green building covered in advertisements about its great deals. One red sign against the window reads GUITARS WANTED. Two tall buildings dwarf it on both sides, white and black graffiti across their walls. I hurry inside.

A little bell rings as the door opens and shuts. Guitars hang on the walls—some of them sparkling blue, some of them regular wood. There are other instruments as well: mandolins like the ones in Greece, and banjos that look like pictures I've seen online.

The owner watches me over a car magazine. He's heavyset, with thinning brown hair, even though he's not that old. I pick my way around the stuff.

"Um, excuse me, sir?" I reach the counter, but it's almost as tall as me. I can see more of the glass-enclosed amps and guitar pick selection than of the owner.

"You after something particular, boy?" The man flips a page of his magazine, but he doesn't look away.

"I'm trying to find a rebab. It's, um, an Afghan instrument—sort of has a boatlike base?" I outline the shape in the air with my hands. "It's a long-neck lute with three main strings, two drone ones, and thirteen sympathetic. My baba—um, grandfather's—was stolen."

The owner nods, and he bends behind the counter. "Something like that came in recently."

He straightens, and I cannot breathe. He's holding the rebab. *Our* rebab. There are the familiar inlaid patterns of ivory and ebony along the base, the mother-of-pearl bright against the neck's reddish wood, the beaded tassel hanging off the chipped pegbox.

It's Baba's rebab.

I lean up and reach.

"Hold on. I'm not running a charity shop." The man moves it away. He narrows his eyes. "This is a good instrument. It's going for . . . seven hundred dollars."

"Seven hundred dollars?" My mouth dries. "But it was stolen!"

"Not my fault. You got seven hundred dollars?"

I shake my head. This can't be right, but I don't know enough about the law to protest more.

"Well then." The man shifts in his chair and leans to put the rebab back.

"Wait!" I lick my lips. *Seven hundred dollars!* Baba barely makes enough to pay rent. All I own is my backpack and a few odds and ends. How do kids make money in America? "It's a family heirloom. I can get the money."

The man studies me with a shrewd eye. He reminds me of the vendors at the market, examining every customer for their weakness.

Seven hundred dollars! plays on repeat in my head. How will I get seven hundred dollars? I don't know. I'll have to plan the how later. But right now what matters is that I *will*. I clench my jaw and make myself meet his gaze without squirming. I can make the money—I *can*. If I believe it, so will he.

Finally, he lifts his eyebrows. "Okay, kid. You have four weeks."

My held breath whooshes out of me. "And you'll take down the ad from the internet?"

"Sure. Whatever." He shrugs. "I expect seven hundred dollars by July 5, or this goes right back on display."

"Yes, all right—thank you!" I make for the exit. I need to think, but right now I'm too dizzy with hunger and hope. Twenty-eight days from now is just before Eid al-Fitr, July 6, the end of Ramadan. At least, assuming the crescent moon is sighted then—if it's cloudy or the predictions are off, it could be a day later. If I get the rebab for Eid, it would make the perfect gift.

It isn't until I step outside, into a cold drizzle, that I return to reality.

I have nothing—no money, no valuables, no skills— and I need to make seven hundred dollars in one month.

If I don't, the rebab will be gone forever.

5

THE MIDDLE SCHOOL CAFETERIA ALWAYS MAKES ME
wish for the school in Istanbul. We often shared meals
there, seated on the ground, with little to give. But most
important, it was *quiet*.

Here, sound beats on my head in waves, so loud I
hardly hear my own thoughts. All the voices merge into
a roar, and the roar bounces around until it bleeds off the
walls and pools in my ears.

I sit cross-legged at the table in the farthest corner,
which I've been using since my first day. The smell from
the food line is less overwhelming here, and it's slightly
quieter than the center of the room. I set my backpack
on the bench beside me and pull out my phone while the
rest of the class gets their meals. I've already explained
to the teacher—Mrs. Mulligan—about Ramadan, so

she doesn't pester me to get food. She's sitting a few tables away, where she has a good view of everyone, and sometimes I catch her glancing toward me.

Keeping my phone under the table—I'm not fully sure yet whether it's allowed, even at lunch break—I click into the note-taking app. It's been two days since I found the rebab at the music shop, and I've been racking my brain for ideas to get seven hundred dollars. So far all I've been able to do is write this:

How to make $700:
- Gardening?
- Job? (I think that might be illegal here?)
- Concert? (If I had the rebab . . .)
- Sell something?
- Exchange coins for USD? (Afghanis: 2, Iranian rial: 1, euros [Turkey and Greece]: 5) Not worth much!
- ??????

The list was small to begin with, but every time I check again it seems to shrink. Baba always made sure we only owned as much as we could carry in my backpack, his rebab case, and a small suitcase. All of my belongings—toothbrush, a few shirts, some trousers, one pair of shoes—I need. There's nothing to sell.

Someone dumps a tray on my table, and I jump, nearly losing my phone. Dan plops down across from me.

"This is the weird corner, you know," he says, as if we're in the middle of a conversation. He has to shout over the noise. "See the stain on the ceiling? People say a teacher's body was stuffed up there after she was murdered."

I glance up. The stain is too light and tan to have been blood. Water damage, more likely. I don't tell Dan, though. His food—a quesadilla and a fruit cup, according to today's menu—makes my stomach rumble. Digging my palm into the space below my ribs, I swallow and glance away. My head swims with hunger.

"You don't say much," Dan observes, starting to eat. "How'd it go at the music store? Did you get the thing back?"

"No, ah . . ." I shift my gaze to the table. "The owner said he would sell it to me for seven hundred dollars. I have a month to get the money for him."

"*Seven hundred dollars?*" Dan whips out his phone and starts swiping. "It was only listed for five hundred!"

My stomach sinks. So much for being a good bar-terer. I must have shown the owner I was desperate, that

I would agree to anything. There's no way I can talk down the price now.

"Ugh, I can't find the ad for some reason. But I swear it was five hundred dollars yesterday."

"He promised to take the ad off eBay," I say. At least he did that much.

"What a jerk." Dan puts his phone away. "Are you going to come play soccer today?"

I open my mouth to say no, but before I can, a group from our grade walks up to the table. The tall boy leads them. He throws his tray down next to me and sits. He and his friends are complaining loudly about something, but between the roaring room and their quick words, I can't translate fast enough to understand.

"So, what're we doing here?" The tall one turns to Dan as he asks the question, so I can see his face enough to piece his words together. He glances at my key chain. "Hey, that's cool."

"Guys, this is Sami." Dan points to me. "Sami, this is Justin, Mike, and Peter. I'm trying to add Sami for offense at the rec center."

"Ah! Gonna replace me, then?" Peter, the tall one, asks. He laughs, but there's something angry in it.

"No." Dan rolls his eyes. "There's no cap on teams. But we do need someone to fill in until you can play again."

"Hm." Peter starts eating. Around a mouthful, he practically yells in my ear, "Why aren't you eating? You sick or something?"

"No," I try to answer. My voice is swallowed by the chatter. I clear my throat and try again, louder. "No. I'm Muslim. It's Ramadan."

"Ramen-what?" Justin hollers across the table.

"It's a month of fasting." It feels like I might as well be yelling into a sandstorm. They're all staring at me blankly. I tug my backpack closer and scoot to make more space between me and Peter. My Manchester United key chain clangs on the metal bench. "We don't eat or drink while the sun is up, and then we break the fast every evening."

"Yeah, okay." Peter looks at my key chain. "Where did you get that?"

I take the key chain and rub the metal between my thumb and forefinger, steadying myself. Between the noise and the food, I'm nearly dazed. "Oh, um, Athens."

"Where's that?"

For a moment, I'm not sure if he's joking. But he stares at me expectantly. "Greece."

"Where's that?"

"Come on, Pete," Dan explodes. "It's in Europe. *Duh.*"

Peter glares across the table. "*I* knew that. Just seeing if *he* did."

Dan snorts. I glance between them. When Peter and his group sat down at the table, I thought they were Dan's friends. But the others are busy cramming food into their mouths, and the air across the table has gone tight. My pulse pounds in my head. I don't want any part of this—I wish they hadn't sat here.

"England's in Europe." Peter turns to me like nothing's happened. "Manchester United is in England. You willing to sell that key chain? I've got two dollars."

I'm shaking my head before he even stops talking, my fingers closed around the key chain. The cold metal warms against my palm. *No*, I'm about to say. *Never.*

I'm sure Baba paid more than two dollars for it—everything is more expensive in Greece—and we never had a lot left after the bribes and travel and food. To give it to me, he wrapped it in a page of notebook paper, with some string tied around for a ribbon. While I opened the package, he bounced his knees with excitement, and when I tugged it free, he started to chant, "Hello! Hello! We are the Busby Boys!"

He'd grabbed the rebab and plucked a few notes as we chanted together. Other men sharing our hostel room joined in. The victory cry rose and rose until it burst into pure celebration. I laughed until my ribs hurt, and Baba had to wipe tears from his eyes.

That was one of the only days on our journey when I felt a little like I was home.

"Then how about a trade?" Peter goes on. He digs in his backpack and pulls out a small blue iPod. "You want this?"

"Jeez, Pete!" Dan gasps. "You could buy the key chain yourself for five dollars on eBay. That iPod's worth way more!"

"The key chain is from *Europe*, idiot. That makes it extra cool." Peter waves the iPod at me. "What do you say?"

Even with Peter's excuse, it seems a strange trade. Why would the key chain be worth so much just because I got it in Europe? To me it's worth a lot because of the look on Baba's face when he gave it to me. I'd never trade that memory for anything.

Seven hundred dollars echoes in my hollow head. Suddenly my brain feels as empty as my stomach. The key chain weighs heavily against my palm. *Twenty-six days.* My dry throat aches. Is the memory of Baba giving me the key chain worth more than the rebab? What else do I have to get it back? A few coins. A possibility of jobs.

I don't have a choice. If I can sell or trade the iPod, I'll be that much closer to having the money.

I unhook the key chain from my backpack. "Okay."

Peter swaps with me. The iPod isn't as heavy as my key chain. Gunk blocks my voice, and it won't go away, even when I clear my throat.

Dan frowns at Peter.

Peter and his friends ignore me, talking about scrubbing graffiti and then sports while they take huge bites of food. I don't try to translate. I'm a hole in the noise—a silence so heavy I can hardly hear anything over it.

Then they leave to put their trays away. I finally look down at the iPod in my hand and press the on button.

Nothing happens.

Panic pricks my neck, but I push it down. My cousin in Iran had an iPod. He used it to listen to English audiobooks. Sometimes, when the charge got low, he just had to press longer. I try again.

Nothing. Not even the warning flash of a battery sign.

Maybe it's just so low it won't even turn on until it's charged. Except I don't have a charger. I don't have any way to know—

I look up just as Peter and his two friends go past. Peter's smiling. Not like a kid. Like one of the smugglers.

Like the smuggler who yanked me onto a black boat, assuring Baba that it was the highest quality, the best option, while he pocketed all our money and the cheap plastic groaned under my feet. His smile hid the lie.

Peter is past me now, but I saw it: the lie and the win.

The iPod in my hand is broken.

TRADE LOG

Days: 26

THINGS TO TRADE:

iPod (broken)

COMPLETED TRADES:

1. Manchester United key chain -> iPod

6

AFTER THE LAST BELL, I HEAD TO THE SCHOOL parking lot, my bones still aching with the silence. I've changed my list of ideas to a trade log, but all it shows is my mistake: *iPod (broken)*. Kids jostle me in the hallway, but I just absorb the hits and nudges.

When I step into the mid-afternoon sun, Dan squeezes between me and the door and grabs my backpack to pull me outside, free of the crush.

"What'd Pete do?" he says.

"Nothing," I answer automatically. I'm ready to shrug it off and slip away. I don't want any trouble. I don't want to ask for any help. People like Peter just get worse if you try to stand up to them. And people rarely help without expecting something in return.

Dan shakes his head. "No *way* he actually traded an iPod for that key chain, even if it is from Europe."

My phone buzzes. I fish it out of my pocket. "Sorry—just a minute."

It's a text from Baba: *Working late. Will bring home dinner, inshallah.*

He's used a chicken-leg icon. I taught him how to find the emojis during a downpour in Athens, to distract him from worrying that the moisture in our cheap hostel room would warp the rebab's wood.

Baba and the rebab. I promised myself I'd get it back. Dan might know how to help—he did find the rebab again in the first place—and even if he does want something in return, so what? I'm at a dead end.

I take a deep breath. "Peter's iPod is broken," I say, reaching for it. "At least, I think it is. It won't turn on."

"What a loser. Here, give it." Dan takes a rectangular portable charger and a white cord from his backpack. He plugs in the iPod. "This should work."

We both lean closer, watching for any sign of life.

The iPod does nothing. How could I have been so *stupid*?

"Sometimes, if it's really, really, *really* low, it takes a half hour to work again," Dan says. When he glances at me, he's trying to hide a smile—and failing. "I guess you'll just have to come to soccer practice. I'll leave it hooked up in my backpack, and it'll be charged by the end."

"Oh." I fidget with my backpack straps. I mostly want to retreat to my apartment. But a part of me is actually sort of curious. I haven't played soccer in so long. And I do need the iPod to charge.

"Okay," I say, but it comes out hesitant and weak. I clear my throat. With more certainty this time: "Okay."

"Come on," Dan calls, waving me into the rec center's courtyard. "It's going to be awesome!"

My hand closed around the scar on my arm, I slip through the gate without lifting my gaze to the razor wire. Even under my sleeves, I can trace the long, puckered groove. The wire snagged my skin at the Iran border, and to keep silent, I bit my lip so hard it bled. When Baba touched my arm in the dark, he thought I had spilled water on myself. He didn't even realize I had been cut until morning.

Teenagers play American football on the tarmac, not paying us any notice. I peel my fingers off the scar and hurry to catch up with Dan.

"Do you think Ms. Nolan has a mustache?" Dan asks suddenly, spinning around so he's walking backward. He sticks a finger under his nose to demonstrate.

"I—um— No?" To be honest, I haven't looked our language arts teacher directly in the eyes since I came to the school.

Dan sighs and lets his hand fall. "I think she does. I can't *stop* thinking about it. If I fail the year-end tests, it'll be because her mustache was so distracting."

Mention of the tests makes my empty stomach turn. The agency said I have some flexibility, since I only just transferred. But they also said I scored on target with the students my age, and I don't want to be held back a year. I don't want to stick out as the oldest in class.

"Only twelve days left!" Dan grabs the front door and throws it open. "Then we're free!"

I barely catch its handle before it starts to swing shut. *Free.* There are a lot worse places to be trapped than in a school. But I didn't know that a few years ago, when I used to complain to Mor about classes. So I'm not surprised Dan thinks that way now.

A bell chirps when we walk into the rec center's lobby. The light from the windows reflects off the white walls, making the space airy and bright. Somewhere people must be running, because I can hear sneakers squeaking on a polished floor. Upbeat music plays quietly in the background.

"Hello!" calls the lady behind the desk, cutting off a

conversation she was having with a tall man. Her skin is paler than the photoshopped advertisements in Kabul. "How are you today, Dan?"

"Pretty well, Juniper. Hi, Coach." Dan grabs a clipboard and scribbles something down.

"Hey, Dan. You're on time, which probably means I'm late." The man straightens from leaning on the desk and pulls his gym bag out of the way. His voice dips with an accent in a way that makes me think of hot summers and brown fields. I might have heard that sort of voice before in the camps. East African, maybe? "It was nice talking to you, Juniper."

"Have a good practice," she says, clicking the pen in her hand about ten times before she puts it down. Pushing her red hair behind her ear, she turns to me. "Hi there. Who are you?"

"Sami," I answer, approaching the desk.

Dan passes me the clipboard. "He's gonna join my team."

Coach lifts his bag's strap onto his shoulder, but something heavy inside shifts, and a few magazines tumble onto the floor. The covers are all animated characters punching each other or jumping off planes.

Miss Juniper stands. "What—"

"Oh, da—" Coach starts to say, but cuts himself off.

Kneeling to grab the magazines, he adds quickly, "It's fine—I've got it."

Dan's already scooping them up. He pauses to examine each of the covers, his grin getting wider and wider. I stand aside, still holding the clipboard.

"I didn't know you had *Game Informer*!" Dan exclaims, lifting a magazine with a boy in a green costume wielding a sword. "That's, like, my *favorite*."

"Yeah, it's cool." Coach takes Dan's gatherings. They start to slip when he grabs his bag, and he shifts them against his chest awkwardly. Laughing, his ears red under his dark skin, he says, "See you inside. Bye, Juniper."

"Bye!" Miss Juniper sits again, tugging on the chain of her necklace.

I look back down at the clipboard. Dan's written his name and the time we arrived, so I copy him and add mine. Under a column labeled *Activities*, Dan's written *SOCCER*.

"I wish I could get *Game Informer*," Dan tells Miss Juniper. "My dad used to give me his old copies when he was done with them. *So* cool. Oh, just write *soccer* there, Sami."

"You know," Miss Juniper says, "we do have tutors who could help you prep for your tests, and even some music programs . . ."

"No," Dan says, flat and blunt. "Just. Soccer."

She shakes her head but laughs. "Okay, okay. Your friend might want to try some other things, though, so I just thought I'd put it out there. Is he your new offense?"

"Yeah, looks like Pete's detention-bound for the rest of the school year."

I stop writing. Peter. *Pete.* The boy who traded me the broken iPod is the same boy who sold the bracelet and did the graffiti. So he's stuck in detention while I'm playing on his soccer team. No wonder he hates me. No wonder the trade backfired.

When I pass the clipboard back to Miss Juniper, her necklace flashes in the sunlight. It's gold with a charm at the end.

No, not a charm. It's a twenty-cent euro coin.

I didn't know people here made coins into jewelry. Miss Juniper has other things on her desk, too—her pencil holder is a cup with a map on it, her mouse pad shows the Eiffel Tower, and a travel book with pages marked by colorful tabs sits next to her keyboard.

"Okay, you're good to go!" Miss Juniper says. "Have fun! Sami, come see me after practice and I'll have a few forms for you to give your parents."

"All right." I don't point out that I have no parents. My head's still whirling at the sight of her necklace.

"Thanks!" Dan takes off down the hallway, and I have to run to catch up with him.

But I don't mind. For a second, I forget about the failure of my first trade.

Because Miss Juniper wants to travel, and I have currency.

TRADE LOG

Days: 26

THINGS TO TRADE:

iPod (broken)

Coins—Afghanis: 2, Iranian rial: 1, euros
(Turkey and Greece): 5 (Miss Juniper?)

COMPLETED TRADES:

1. Manchester United key chain -> iPod

7

AHEAD OF ME, DAN SHOULDERS INTO A SWINGING DOOR. The squeaking sneakers and echoing shouts get louder, cavernous. I pause a step inside. The court is huge, with basketball hoops on either end. Orange cones separate the two halves. To my left is a group of younger kids goofing off while an adult calls names. To my right, Coach is leading a team in warm-up stretches. Dan throws his backpack against the wall—my iPod still hooked to the portable charger inside—and runs to join them.

I hang back, suddenly unsure about all this. The team members cast me curious glances, and they're not just boys—there are three girls. They're mingled in the group, and one—a girl with beads in her hair—watches me with open curiosity while she stretches her arms toward the ceiling. My head goes hot, and I drop my gaze to the court floor.

I've heard of girls skateboarding and biking, and sometimes my girl cousins would kick a ball around on the flat roofs of our homes. But they were always fully covered and never on a team like this. I'm not surprised that girls and boys both play soccer in America, but being expected to play with girls still fills me with a rush of unease and embarrassment—like missing a step on the stairs.

"Hello, Dan, Sami," Coach says, lowering his arms. "Come on over. Dan, do you want to introduce—?"

Dan jumps right in. "Hey, everyone, this is my friend Sami."

Friend.

I blink at Dan. He says it—*friend*—lightly, freely. How can he mean that? He barely knows me. I certainly don't feel like I know him.

In Afghanistan, before the wedding, friends also came to me easily and swiftly. There is an Afghan proverb: The first day you meet, you are friends. The next day you meet, you are brothers.

But now, in the *after*, how can I ever be sure there will be a "next day"?

Dan lines up with the others and waves me over. A few of the kids call greetings to me. I join them, and

Coach resumes the stretches. I try to follow along as we stand on one leg, then reach for the floor, then roll our heads around (my neck cracks when I do). Every move comes stiff and awkward, and I'm sure all the others are noticing when I lean too slowly or lift the wrong arm. My jeans don't let me stretch as far as the kids wearing shorts, but I don't have a change of clothes. Last, Coach has us jog around the gym. I love to run fast, but I hang back with Dan near the middle of the group. My sneakers smack against the hard floor.

The rhythm of our footfalls pounds in my head, and my fingers itch for the rebab's strings—for some way to find the song I hear in the beat. But my hands are empty. The melody stays hidden.

When we finish the lap, Coach brings us to the center. "All right. Today we're going to work on passes. At the end of practice, we'll do a short game. Okay?"

Dan hoots, and others bounce on the balls of their feet. I stick my hands in my pockets.

Though I try to concentrate on Coach's instructions about passing, I keep getting distracted. The girl with beads braided into her dark hair stands in front, a little space between her and the others. Whenever she shifts, the beads clink together. Every time it happens, I lose track of what Coach is saying.

Dan leans over to me. "Layla"—he points to the bead

girl—"is the best on offense. Even better than Pete. She rocks."

We run through the practice routines, and then Coach counts us into two teams to play the mock game. He passes out blue and red mesh shirts, to help make the sides clear. Two of the girls go on the other team—one of them ("Julie," Dan whispers) taller than all of us, with her wiry black curls pulled under a headband, and the other ("Hamida," I'm told) with long bangs she has to keep pushing back. Layla is put on our team—which Dan has dubbed the Tornado Sharks—and Dan gives me a big thumbs-up like we've won already.

I stumble through most of the game. The floor doesn't feel right under my feet, and the ball skids too quickly across the polished wood. We're tied as we enter the last three minutes.

I'm up the court when Dan passes the ball to Layla. A defender on the other team rushes her. She searches for an opening and spots me.

"Sami!" she shouts, kicking the ball so hard it lifts off the floor.

The ball soars straight to me. I hold my hands out of the way and bounce it off my chest. As soon as it hits the floor, I run it toward the goal. I almost trip on my first step and almost lose the ball on the second. But then my pace evens, and I find my rhythm. The ball moves with me instead of trying to slide away. It's like a song—one that I've forgotten but my muscles remember.

Another defender comes at me. I see Layla out of the corner of my eye and pass the ball to the middle of the court. One of the other kids goes after it, but Layla intercepts first. She's waving me on, and I run toward the goal, my eyes never leaving the ball. The kids between us part for a second, and she kicks. I stop the ball and turn toward the goal.

I'm through the penalty area. Two defenders close in on either side, and the goalkeeper sprints forward to block me. I drive the ball straight at the keeper. He catches it in his hands and lifts it to toss. Layla's bright beads flash to my right. The keeper throws, but too low. I dive for the ball, hitting it with my head and knocking it crossways across the penalty area. Layla is right where I need her— she kicks the ball toward the net. For a moment everything goes quiet . . .

And then the ball hits the net with a satisfying *swish*.

All the sounds of the gym return with a roar. Dan jumps on me, screaming like we've just won a championship, and soon the rest of the Tornado Sharks join in, Layla among them.

She punches me in the arm. "Nice header!"

"That was amazing!" I gasp, out of breath.

"This deserves a selfie!" Dan pulls his phone from his pocket and leans in, stretching out his arm. Layla backs up a step, so it can be just me and Dan, but he says, "Get in!"

Grinning, Layla throws an arm around my shoulders and gives a thumbs-up. Next to her in the preview, I'm pale—though not nearly as pale as Dan. He might as well be a ghost. Giddy happiness bubbles in my chest, and I laugh, not even looking at the screen.

The phone makes a camera sound, and Dan brings it close to look. "That's a new profile pic right there."

"Send it to me!" Layla says.

I look over her shoulder as she pulls the picture up on her phone. My breath hitches in my throat. In the image, my smile is wide and open. It's my plar jan's smile. Pashtun men don't normally smile in pictures, so I had no record of his smile—I had forgotten the way he held his head back and his eyes scrunched up. But here it is, in my own face.

I had *forgotten*.

"Great job, everyone," Coach says above the chatter. "Awesome teamwork! Our time's up now, but I'll see you all tomorrow. Have a good rest of the day!"

The kids jostle past me to gather their stuff, and

I remember the real reason I'm here. I rub away the sting in my eyes with the palms of my hands, then turn around to Dan. "Do you think the iPod's charged enough?"

"Oh, right!" Dan sprints to his backpack, and I follow. He grabs the iPod and charger. I watch while he holds down the power button.

Nothing.

"Hm. It's not the battery," Dan says. My heart sinks. I traded the key chain for nothing.

Dan must see the expression on my face, because he adds, "It's okay; I have another idea." Dan looks around at the other kids grabbing their backpacks. "Benj, do you have a guitar pick?"

"Um, probably?" The goalie from the other mini-team drags his red backpack next to Dan's and digs around. "What do you need it for?"

"Magic," Dan says loftily.

I glance between the two of them, trying to keep my confusion hidden. If the iPod's too broken to charge, what else can Dan do?

Benj finds a black guitar pick and tosses it to Dan. "You have to give it back. Hamida's brother loaned it to me."

"I just need it for a second."

To me, Benj adds, "Hey, sweet move for the score. Where'd you learn that?"

"Around." It feels too complicated to say in Istanbul—that will only lead to more questions.

Dan catches my eye. "Sami, can you ask Coach for a business card?"

"Um—all right." I step away, uncertain, then jog off. I find Coach finishing packing his gym bag with the soccer balls. Layla's been helping, and they're talking about something when I reach them.

"That was some fancy work, Sami," Coach says, spotting me. He zips his bag shut. "Glad to have you on the team. Have you recently moved to the area?"

"Thank you—and yes. Just this month." I swallow on my dry throat so my voice won't rasp. I'm more thirsty after the exercise, and I will not be able to drink until sunset at eight o'clock.

"Where are you from originally?" Coach asks.

"Afghanistan." He looks surprised, but I press on before he can say anything. "Do you have—a business card? Dan asked."

"Not for myself," Coach says, even more puzzled.

"I don't think that matters." I look over my shoulder. Dan's doing something I can't see, but other team members have gathered around him.

"Okay, well, I have this." Coach stands and takes a wallet from his back pocket. He tugs a card free and offers it. The paper feels flimsy. The design is pretty simple: just white paper with black text.

"Thanks!" I say again, turning around.

Layla follows me at a trot back toward the others. "Hey, ah, what are you guys up to?"

I falter, my neck heating and my tongue going itchy. "Just . . . trying to fix something."

Dan's amassed a small crowd. I squeeze around Benj and another kid to see what he's doing. He has the iPod open so the insides show. My heart flops down to the pit of my stomach. I didn't tell Dan to take it apart!

"Whoa," Layla says.

"Dan pried it open with a guitar pick," Benj tells her.

"Got a card?" Dan reaches toward me without looking up.

I pass the card to him, not sure what to say or do. Silver squares and circles dot the shining green plastic, the patterns almost like a city map. A narrow orange-and-black ribbon connects the back of the iPod to the front. Exposed, it seems fragile.

"Perfect." Dan puts the iPod down and folds the card. He licks the edge and tugs the paper apart in a narrow strip.

Layla slips around the other side of Benj. "Gross!"

"Is that your iPod?" Benj asks Dan.

"Nope. Sami's."

"For real?" Benj glances at me skeptically. Then he sighs. "I've been wanting one *forever*. My *abuela* only speaks Spanish, and my Spanish is worse than her English. If I had an iPod, I could download lessons onto it. I did all the research and everything, but my aunt *still* says it's too expensive. How'd you get this one?"

"Traded." I lean in to watch while Dan tears the small rectangle into a smaller square. I hesitate, but add, "If Dan can fix it, I was hoping to trade it for something else."

"Like what?" Benj asks quickly. "I've got stuff."

I'm not sure what I'd want to trade for, but then, I'm not even sure the iPod will be tradable. "Well, nothing in particular. I won't know till I see, probably."

"You'll be here tomorrow? I'll take pictures of my stuff at home tonight. Then you can see them after practice, and we can decide on a swap. Yeah?"

I nod, but I'm not really listening. Dan's stuck the square of paper against one of the pieces inside the iPod, and now he's carefully putting it back together.

He holds up the guitar pick without lifting his head. "Here, Benj, take this."

Benj retrieves the pick. I crouch beside Dan, holding my breath.

"Here we go . . ." He presses the circle button and the on button at the same time.

Black screen.

Then it turns blue, and the Apple logo flashes.

"Eureka!" Dan shouts, fist-pumping the air. "Magic Dan does it again!"

I carefully take the iPod from him while Layla and Benj lean in to get a better look, pummeling Dan with questions. My fingers tremble, but for once it's not the hunger or the sadness that's gnawing my insides.

It's a painful warmth. Hope.

TRADE LOG

Days: 26

THINGS TO TRADE:

iPod (repaired!!)

Coins—Afghanis: 2, Iranian rial: 1, euros

(Turkey and Greece): 5 (Miss Juniper?)

COMPLETED TRADES:

1. Manchester United key chain -> iPod

8

THE NEXT DAY, BABA AND I ARE PUTTING ON OUR sandals after the Friday service and prayer at the Islamic Society of Boston Cultural Center. The shoe cubbies are on both sides of a long atrium, the men's on the left and the women's on the right. Behind Baba, people linger in the bright room under the dome, talking and laughing. Baba has been quiet. It's become almost normal since the rebab was taken—Baba's strange quiet.

"I think I'll go to practice at the rec center again this afternoon," I say in Pashto. I want to see what Benj will have to offer for a trade, but it's true when I add, "I might keep going regularly, you know? It's kind of fun."

Baba slips the strap over his heel before he answers. "So, you like your team?"

I nod. "Dan's cool—though, well . . . enthusiastic.

And Benj seems nice. And Layla's a great player." I wiggle to my feet and hold a hand out for Baba. "Though it's *strange* playing indoors instead of on the street or rooftops."

With a soft chuckle, Baba lets me help him stand. "Ah, Sami, we are in a new world. Best get used to it."

His eyes don't crinkle. And his mouth loses the momentary almost-grin. The sadness seeps into his silences.

My plar had silences like that. Seeing Baba's stooped shoulders and loose hands brings back a memory I'd nearly lost, sudden and vivid and painfully bright.

I walked into the living room where my plar sat on a toshak, feet flat against the floor instead of legs crossed. He stared down at the cell phone in one hand, his other hand worked into his hair, his glasses sliding slowly down his nose. He didn't push them up. The Taliban had called. Again. I sat beside him, leaning to check what his phone said. It was blank, our reflections gray in the glass. My plar put his arm around my shoulder. His hand was too tight.

Did he smell like dust or like chai? Was the phone cracked, or was it new? I think he had just changed the number.

But I can't remember more than that image—the memory slides out of my brain slick as a snake over sand. It's gone, like the rebab.

Baba walks on toward the mosque's exit, past the coffee shop—closed for Ramadan—and the other people. The imam stands near the door to say farewells as the congregation leaves. Baba stops to speak with him. I hang back, still thinking about Plar.

"Hello?"

A man has stopped in front of me, smiling with a friendly crooked tilt to his mouth. His smile and well-trimmed beard look familiar

He chuckles. "You have an intense stare. Do you know that?"

"Oh." I shake my head.

"Farid." He offers me a hand. "Farid Wazir. We haven't actually been introduced. I didn't realize you attended this mosque."

"Sami Safi." I shake his hand, trying to remember why I recognize him.

"I've missed seeing you and your grandfather in Harvard Station. It was wonderful to hear a traditional Afghan instrument on my way home from work. Much better than the opera singer." He makes a face.

It clicks—he's the man who gave us twenty dollars, just before the rebab was taken. "Thank you," I say. "We've missed it, too."

"Uncle Farid!" someone calls. A girl my age comes running up. "Oh! Hi, Sami."

"Hi," I say. She tucks her bangs back under her hijab, and I realize it's one of the girls from the team. "Hamida?" It comes out as a question, and I wince.

She nods. "Yep!" Then she turns to Mr. Farid. "Here's my sketch from today."

I get a glimpse as Mr. Farid turns it this way and that. In pencil, Hamida's drawn an intricate geometric pattern worthy of framing.

"This is very good," Mr. Farid says, giving me a full view. "Don't you think, Sami?"

"Yes," I readily agree.

Hamida looks pleased. "It'd look better if I had a set of Prismacolor markers. Or gel pens. Or charcoal, even. My parents are convinced I'm going to be an engineer, so they don't need to buy me *real* supplies. Cliché, right? But Uncle Farid thinks there might be hope for me."

"You *might* be in for some new art supplies when your birthday comes around." Mr. Farid smiles, passing back the drawing.

Hamida rolls her eyes. "That's *months* away!"

Baba has finished talking to the imam and turned back to me.

"Assalamu alaikum," Mr. Farid greets him.

"Walaikum assalam," Baba answers in kind.

"Baba," I say, "this is Mr. Farid Wazir and his niece,

Hamida. He used to pass us on his commute. Mr. Farid, Hamida, this is my grandfather, Habibullah Safi."

"I was just getting to know your grandson," Mr. Farid says. "I'm a big fan of your music."

The wrinkles across Baba's forehead deepen, but he bows his head graciously. "Thank you. Music is our joy."

"I have not seen you in some time. I suppose you found a more stable job?" Mr. Farid asks with genuine curiosity. "Street performance isn't always the most steady way to earn a living, though practical ways are probably less enjoyable."

Baba's jaw tightens, and he stares at the floor. My own heart burns thinking of Baba washing dishes instead of playing the rebab. The silence stretches until I think I might burst.

"Baba found something, yes. But, ah, I'm afraid we need to be going. I have soccer practice and Baba has work."

Mr. Farid glances at Baba, his expression confused. "I hope you both have a good week, then. Perhaps you can join us on Sunday—several members will be gathering at Kennedy Greenway for some games before iftar."

"Thank you," Baba says softly, nodding. "We would be honored to join you."

Mr. Farid holds out his hand to shake Baba's. "May you find peace in Ramadan, inshallah."

"Inshallah," I echo. Baba mouths the word, releasing Mr. Farid's hand.

"You're going to practice?" Hamida asks. "We could walk together."

"No, um, I'll be a minute," I answer, my neck heating.

"Okay, then—see you there!" She waves and runs ahead.

Holding Baba's arm, I walk him to the exit. He barely lifts his gaze until we're on the sidewalk outside. I want to say something to make his shame and sorrow leave—something to make him proud and happy again, to remind him he is not only a dishwasher. But what can you say when you have nothing? When even your music has been taken from you?

I consider telling him the truth about the rebab and the trades. But his pride would be hurt, and he would insist on getting it himself. He's already working so hard, and the loss of the rebab isn't his responsibility—it's mine. The only way to redeem my mistake is to recover it myself and give it as a gift on Eid al-Fitr.

"I'm sorry," I mutter. "I'm sorry I lost the rebab."

"Sami jan," Baba whispers. "It's not your fault."

He presses his lips together and then tilts my head

down so he can kiss my hair. His words are meant to comfort away the stinging in my throat. But his arm is heavy around my shoulders, and silence falls between us, just like it did with my plar.

My plar knew, I feel. He knew he would die. That's what his silence meant.

I look at Baba, a raging, breaking, tearing question taking shape in my mind—a question that I'm terrified to let fully form.

Will I lose Baba like I lost Plar?

"Have a good practice," Baba says gently. "I will see you tonight, inshallah."

"Inshallah." I nod. He goes the other way.

I don't move until he's disappeared around the corner.

TRADE LOG
Days: 25

THINGS TO TRADE:
iPod (repaired!!)
Coins—Afghanis: 2, Iranian rial: 1, euros
(Turkey and Greece): 5 (Miss Juniper?)

COMPLETED TRADES:
1. Manchester United key chain -> iPod

9

SCHOOL ONLY HAS A HALF DAY ON FRIDAYS, SO I DON'T need to go back to class—I can just go straight to soccer practice. When I reach the rec center, Dan is waiting in the courtyard, hopping on one foot, then the other. I knew I was late, but I didn't realize Dan would be waiting for me.

"What *took* so long?" Dan calls while I'm still on the other side of the fence. He waves his phone, pointing at a text. "Hamida got here *ages* ago, but Julie's going out with her family, so we need you to make the teams even."

"Ages?" How fast was she running?

"Five minutes. Whatever. Come on!"

I quicken to a sprint, and some of the sadness sheds off me. "What did Coach have you work on?"

"Just more passes." Dan hurries me inside, bouncing

around like a dog herding sheep. "Everyone wanted to practice their heading and chest-bouncing after what you did, so we also played with that. Benj almost got a black eye. It was awesome!"

Miss Juniper looks up from her travel book when the door dings. She smiles. "Hello, Sami. Good to see you again. Did your parents get a chance to sign those permission forms?"

"Oh! I forgot." I hesitate. "It's okay if my grandfather signs instead, right?"

"Sure." She smiles, absently tapping a finger against her euro necklace. "Just bring them in soon, okay?"

"Yes, miss." The coins are in my backpack, and I'd like to talk to her about them. But Dan's shoving the pen and clipboard into my hands, so I guess I'll discuss a trade after the game. I scribble my name down.

"Dan," Miss Juniper says, "what were those magazines Coach Austin had in his bag yesterday?"

"*Game Informer*? Only the best guides to the best new video games." Dan's momentarily distracted. "It has reviews and game play and features for recent releases."

Miss Juniper laughs, which makes the freckles on her face scrunch into a bigger blob. "That's all? Well, you tell him I'm a pretty big fan of *Zelda*. I'd love to hear what the magazine says about that."

"For real?" Dan grins. "What did you think of the final boss in—"

"Um, Dan?" I pass the clipboard to Miss Juniper, glancing at the clock over her desk.

"*Right!* Soccer!" Dan takes off for the hallway but spins around again. "We're *definitely* talking afterward, Juniper!"

"Got it!" She waves.

I follow Dan into the gym. Everyone's already been divided into teams, and they're practicing bouncing the balls on their heads when we come in. Layla gets three in a row before Dan announces, "Let's go!"

Coach tosses me a mesh shirt and puts us in our positions. Benj catches my eye and mouths, *After.*

I nod. I still need to arrange a trade for the iPod with Benj, too. *What could he have found?* I push the thought away.

Soccer now. Trades later.

After an hour, we wrap up the game in a tie: Tornado Sharks and Grizzly Bear Vampires 6–6.

"All right, everyone, good effort," Coach says, lifting his voice to get our attention. "Have a great weekend, and I'll see you all on Monday. We'll go over dribbling then."

As soon as Coach finishes, Benj runs to his backpack, takes out his phone, and returns to me. "Look—I've got pictures!"

"Hold on. I want to see!" Dan says, joining us.

We all lean over Benj's phone together. Benj narrates as he flicks through the photos. There's a stack of paperback books (Dan scoffs), a painting of a flower in a cracked frame, an assortment of old T-shirts Benj has outgrown, and a box with three weird-looking small statues (Benj insists they're *figurines*, which as far as I can tell is just a fancier word for small statues). The figurines are kids with pale skin and blue eyes. One is a boy carrying a girl, one is a boy with a fishing pole, and another is two girls whispering together.

"They're made of clay or something," Benj explains. "They're from my great-grandparents—my aunt got them when they died. Anyway, she says they're weird, and she's trying to get rid of them."

I scroll through the pictures once more, unsure if any of this would be useful to me.

Dan's already shaking his head. "Benj, that iPod's probably worth eighty, a hundred dollars. This is just a load of junk."

Benj glares. "Not *junk*. Someone might pay a lot for this stuff."

Dan snorts.

"I'll think about it." I hand Benj his phone. "I can let you know soon."

With a doubtful nod, Benj tucks his phone into his pocket.

"Hey, Sami!" Hamida calls, trotting over. "Let me give you my number—then you can text us if you decide to join us on Sunday."

"Oh." I fish around in my pocket for my phone. "All right."

"Benj, are you still coming?" Hamida asks while she waits.

"Is Omar?"

Hamida rolls her eyes. "Yes, he'll be there with his guitar."

"Then I'm definitely there."

I exchange numbers with Hamida, but I slip away while she chats with Benj. Layla stands by the backpacks alone, texting, but also casting little looks at the team as they pack up and mill around. It reminds me of how I used to type on my phone while I was sitting alone in the cafeteria—trying to look busy. She stands up and pulls on her bag when I approach, and I get the bag of coins from my own backpack before I swing it over my shoulders.

She eyes my hand. "What are those?"

"Coins." I shrug. "I thought Miss Juniper might like to trade for them."

"Trade?" Layla echoes.

"Yeah. I'm trying to—earn extra money." I don't want to talk about the rebab, especially after Baba's silence today.

"Ohh!" Layla exclaims. She leans closer to me and lowers her voice. "Don't trade with *Juniper*. Trade with *Coach*."

I frown at her. Why would I give them to someone who, as far as I can tell, couldn't care less about coins?

"Coach *likes* Juniper," Layla explains, rolling her eyes. "He's been trying to talk to her forever. If you trade him the coins—"

"He can give them to her," I finish, catching on. My mind starts racing. I glance across at Coach. Dan is with him, and I hear him say *gaming* and *Zelda* while Dan helps gather the equipment. "Thanks, Layla!"

If I make a trade with Coach instead of Miss Juniper . . . A plan forms in my mind.

I run over to Coach, coins clutched in my hand. Dan is heading to the wall to grab his backpack. Now or never.

"Coach, ah . . ." I trail off, my face getting hot, suddenly unsure how to say any of this. Even if Layla's right and Coach likes Miss Juniper, that doesn't make it less embarrassing to say.

Coach puts the last soccer ball in his bag and glances at me with his eyebrows raised a little. "Yes, Sami?"

I shake the bag so Coach can see the coins through the plastic. "I—um—Layla thought you might like these? Um, or Miss Juniper might . . . ?"

His face brightens with interest, and he takes the bag. The coins shift as he angles it to examine each. "These are really cool, Sami. Where are they from? I recognize the euro."

"Afghanistan, Iran, Turkey, Greece." I point as I say each country.

Coach whistles. "You've been all those places?" He turns them over, still in the bag. "Why are you giving them away?"

"Well, not . . . giving, exactly." My face grows hotter. "More like a trade. I was wondering if you'd maybe be willing to trade the coins for one of your game magazines?"

With a surprised laugh, Coach kneels by his bag. "Sure. I don't normally keep them long anyway." He takes a pile of eight magazines and offers them to me. "Here you go. One for every coin."

"Thank you!" I take the magazines. Second trade complete.

"Did I see you making a deal with Benj?" Coach asks as he eases the strap over his shoulder and stands. "What are you doing all this trading for, Sami?"

Instead of meeting Coach's eyes, I glance at the magazines' covers. "Oh . . . just . . . trying to get something back."

Before Coach can ask more, Dan joins us. "Wait, what's happening here?" he asks. "How'd you get those?"

"Have a good day, Sami, Dan," Coach says, shifting the gym bag and heading to the exit, the coins still in his hand.

I explain the trade to Dan. His eyes have grown to twice their usual size by the time I'm done. I can't even make my proposal before he cuts in. "I'll trade for those! I'll check tonight. I bet I have something you could use. We've got plenty of stuff lying around."

"Okay." I slip the magazines carefully into my backpack. The gym has emptied by now, and Dan and I leave together.

In the main lobby, Coach is showing Miss Juniper the coins. She's grinning, pushing her red hair aside to get a better look. Layla's at the end of the hall, peering around the corner.

"What are you doing?" Dan asks loudly as we come up to her.

Layla jumps and glares. "I was *trying* to watch, idiot," she retorts. Then she motions to me. "See? Wasn't I right?"

I nod. "Thanks for the tip."

Layla tilts her head, and the beads in her hair clink. "Are you only interested in trading with the team? Or are you open to trades from other places?"

"I want to do more—I just don't know where to look," I answer. "Why?"

Layla grins. "I have an idea."

TRADE LOG

Days: 25

THINGS TO TRADE:

iPod (repaired!!)

Game Informer magazines (Dan)

COMPLETED TRADES:

1. Manchester United key chain -> iPod
2. Coins -> *Game Informer* magazines

10

SATURDAY COMES, AND WHILE BABA IS BUSY WORKING, I find myself on bus 41, arms crossed loosely over my chest. Layla watches out the window and sometimes comments on things we pass, like odd-looking apartments or yards where dogs sit by the gates. As we go farther from Roxbury, the redbrick apartments change to big, fancy houses.

"My mom wants to live in one of those Victorian townhouses, but Dad says that's only going to happen if we find buried treasure." Layla swings her legs, glancing at me and then at the window. "I like our apartment, though. We've lived there pretty much my whole life."

I nod and scoot closer to the edge of the seat. No one else on the bus seems to care that I'm sitting next to her, but I still can't relax. Even though we are classmates, we're not children any longer, and we are not related.

"Why did you live in all those places?" Layla asks suddenly.

"Huh?" I rub my thumb against the scar on my arm, hidden by my sleeve, and try to pay attention.

Layla's looking at the seat in front of us. She presses the sole of her shoe against the back and lets it slide off. "You said you'd been to all those places with the coins. But you haven't just *been* there, right? You lived there."

I watch her put her foot against the seat again. She's not pushing hard enough for the person in front of us to notice—just tapping it. Her question lingers between us. Why did we live in all those places? Because of the war. Because the Taliban tried to kill us. Because my parents died. Because it wasn't safe in Iran. Because Europe sounded better. Because Sergeant Pycior convinced us America would have more opportunities. Because . . . because a lot of reasons that don't actually give an answer.

"I mean, we were refugees, but . . ." I trail off. Words swirl in my head, Pashto and English and Greek. None of them explain it, though. Not really. At last, I say, "I don't know. I don't know why."

She glances at me but doesn't say anything. We sit in silence until we arrive at the bus stop a few minutes later and clamber off together. The street bustles with traffic and Saturday shoppers. Around the corner, someone plays a saxophone. An Indian restaurant is at the end of the block, and the smell of curry makes my empty stomach rumble.

"The shop's right here!" Layla points to a green awning between a noodle restaurant and the Indian bistro.

COBWEBS ANTIQUES & JEWELRY is printed on the window in bold white letters. Flower pots and wire birdcages are arranged outside the door, spilling onto the sidewalk. Layla pats the head of a lion statue as she walks past.

I follow her inside. A bell rings to announce our entrance. Two middle-aged women and an older man standing near the counter on my left look up.

"Hiya, Layla!" the man says, smiling.

"Hi, Mr. Byrne!" Layla squeezes around the women as they resume their conversation, and she makes her way deeper into the room.

I follow, trying to avoid knocking into all of the items haphazardly on display. An antique trunk on the floor has an old map propped against it. A bright red Chinese lantern hangs from the ceiling; its black clumps of string sway above my head. A sheathed dagger sits on a low bookshelf to my right, and old wooden clocks tick on top of a table packed with small decorative boxes. Little framed pieces of paper say *YES* and *YOU DESERVE IT* and *TREAT YOURSELF.*

"My mom normally works downstairs," Layla says over her shoulder.

Sure enough, when we round another bookshelf, a cramped stairway appears. Mirrors and paintings of ladies in large, cloudlike dresses decorate the walls. Chai cups and books sit on the edge of the steps. I keep to the left to avoid accidentally kicking anything.

"Mom!" Layla calls, going to the bottom step and then edging aside to make room for me.

"Oh! Hi, Lay." A woman wearing a bright orange scarf wrapped around her hair rises from behind a counter piled high with odds and ends. "I didn't realize the bus had come already."

"Mom, this is the friend I told you about—Sami." Layla leans against the wall and pokes me. "Sami, this is my mom."

"Call me Michele," Layla's mom says. "I'm so glad you've come by! Layla doesn't normally bring friends over."

There's that word again—*friend*. The "first day" has passed—I've been to the rec center twice this week. Does that mean we're friends? In America, maybe friendship will be different—maybe the word is safer here. Less costly, less vulnerable.

"Nice to meet you." I avoid saying her name, knowing

instantly that I will not be able to call her Michele. In Afghanistan, I was never allowed to address an adult by their first name. I would usually say tra for "aunt" or akaa for "uncle," even if we were not related. But it would be too strange to explain that to Layla's mom.

"Come on back and I'll show you around," Mrs. Michele says, motioning me to enter. "Layla said you might like to explore a bit. You're looking for knickknacks to trade?"

Layla stays where she is, so I hesitantly slip around her and into the room. It's about half the size of the one upstairs, and just as crowded. There are so many items, and all of them so small and colorful and interesting, that it's hard to focus on any one thing. I glance at Layla, but she shows no sign of following.

"So, this is Cobwebs," Mrs. Michele says, spreading her hands to include the mini house statues to her left and the pile of books to her right. "Founded by the lovely Patrick Byrne, who's from Ireland, and the shop is as eccentric as he is. How much has Layla told you about all this?"

"Only a little," I say, half watching while Layla picks up an owl statue the size of her hand and examines it.

"Well, we get a lot of our stuff from estate sales." At my confused expression, she adds, "An estate sale is like a big yard sale—um, market—but in someone's house. Normally they hold them when the owner dies and relatives need to sell his or her belongings."

I glance around again. All these things belonged to *dead* people.

"So we have quite the collection."

"Including those creepy puppets." Layla leans out of the stairwell to point at the far wall. Angry-looking painted puppets hang from pegs just below the ceiling. "Their eyes are weird."

She's not wrong. The puppets' black eyes stare at me when I shift my weight, their half-smiling faces fixed almost in sneers. I tug my sleeves lower over my hands and turn away. Mrs. Michele shakes her head but smiles.

"They're from a collector, and they'll be snatched up soon. Anyway. We've got a back room over here with some new arrivals. Want to see?"

I nod.

"Excellent. Let me show you around some more."

"I'm going to talk with Mr. Byrne," Layla says, slipping up the stairs. "Catch me on your way out, Sami!"

"Okay." I try to push down the uncertainty and shyness creeping over me.

"He'll have her immigrating to Ireland before long," Mrs. Michele says with a laugh. She looks a lot like Layla when she does, though she has faint freckles on her dark cheeks, while Layla's are just plain. "So, this is where I work, mainly, logging inventory and keeping an eye on customers who come downstairs. We have warehouses off-site where our estate purchases go initially, but when we're ready to restock, we bring them here."

She leads me down an even smaller hallway. White lights are strung from the ceiling, and tables covered in lamps are pushed to one wall, while more mirrors are leaned against the other.

It's another basement room, crammed with boxes and furniture. Near the end of the room, my gaze catches on a small statue of the Parthenon sitting on a pile of books. I pause beside it. When I lived in Greece, we could sometimes see the temple on a distant hill, high above the city. In person, it looked more crumbly than this little statue. Someone told me the pollution has damaged it so much you could stick a pencil through one of the columns. Some boys I met in Turkey, who had been held in detention in Greece, said every night they would look at it all lit up from their cell window.

"Cool, isn't it?" Mrs. Michele lifts the Parthenon. "We're just using it as a weight—it's not worth much— but it's a neat piece. Here, you can hold it."

Carefully, I take the miniature. If I put my hands

together, it fits on my open palms. The weight presses down into my skin while I examine it closer, closer than I ever got in person. The air stills, and I can almost smell the exhaust from cars, hear them honking as they rush down the street.

"It's strange how things hold memories," I say, half to myself, half thinking of the rebab. "They almost . . . hide them away for later."

"I know exactly what you mean," Mrs. Michele says.

I glance at her, embarrassed I said anything. But her expression is kind. She absently tucks a tuft of frizzy black hair under her scarf.

"I grew up as an army brat," she explains. "We moved around a lot. There was this certain teddy bear—whenever I hugged it, I'd go straight back to our first move, when I was five years old. Strangest thing." She touches a pair of silk gloves on the table beside us. "I wonder what these hold. It makes them precious, even if no one's here to unlock those times anymore."

My hands shake suddenly, and I almost drop the monument as an image presses up in my head with smothering force:

Shattered glass across the courtyard and the sweet smell of grapes mixed with air on fire—

The almost-memory sits sticky in my head. Without

meaning to, I whisper, "Some memories should stay locked away."

The words sound stupid as soon as they tumble out of my mouth, and my neck gets hot.

Mrs. Michele tilts her head. "Maybe," she says finally. "But in my experience, the memories we try to contain have a way of breaking free. And then they just hurt more."

Anger flares in my chest, so sudden and unexpected that my breath catches. What does she know about painful pasts? Even locked away, the memories claw at my mind, trying to suffocate me in shattered glass and gunpowder smoke. If they weren't contained, they would consume me. But her eyes fog over, and my anger drains away. I know that look. Lots of people have suffered. Not just me.

"Well, so this is room one," Mrs. Michele says with a little laugh. "Come on—let's find out if Mr. Byrne's promised Layla a visa yet."

I put the Parthenon back on the books and follow her. Near the door, I spot something I never expected to see. My heart pounds.

Figurines. Figurines of pale, blond, blue-eyed boys with bicycles and girls carrying baskets.

Just like the ones Benj wants to trade.

Ahead, Mrs. Michele calls back to me, "Are you

coming, Sami? Or did you find something you want to buy?"

"Coming," I say as I hustle to the stairs.

As soon as I catch up, I pull Layla aside while Mrs. Michele speaks with Mr. Byrne. "Do you have Benj's mobile number?" I ask.

"Mobile?" She frowns. "I have his cell."

"Yes—that." I'm so excited, I want to bounce on the balls of my feet. "Can you give it to me?"

"Sure . . ." She takes out her phone, we exchange numbers, and in a minute Benj's contact information appears on my screen.

I send him a text: *Hi, this is Sami. Could you send me a picture of those figurines?*

"Sami, come meet Mr. Byrne," Mrs. Michele says as I slip my phone back into my pocket. We exchange introductions and talk briefly, but the whole time I'm listening for a response from Benj.

My phone dings a few minutes later. Benj has attached his pictures. I glance at Mr. Byrne and clear my throat, uncertain. He looks up from arranging necklaces.

"Ah—I saw some little statues downstairs. They looked like this?" I hold out my phone. "I wondered if you'd buy more, maybe?"

"Mmm." Mr. Byrne flips through the images. "These

are nice Hummel figures. This one's number one hundred forty-three, if I'm not mistaken? Mm-hm. I'd have to see them in person, of course, but I'd probably offer forty or fifty dollars."

I lower my head. I was hoping for more for the iPod—it's the most valuable thing I have.

Mr. Byrne is still looking through the pictures. "Yes, I'd say forty or fifty apiece."

My head pops up. "Really?" I blurt. That would earn me more than one hundred dollars!

"Really." He passes the phone back to me. His eyes are twinkling. "Bring them by and we can work out a deal."

"Yes, sir!"

I type out a quick message to Benj:

Bring your figurines to practice. The trade is on!

TRADE LOG
Days: 24

THINGS TO TRADE:
Game Informer magazines (Dan)

PLANNED TRADES:
iPod for figurines
Figurines for money

COMPLETED TRADES:
1. Manchester United key chain -> iPod
2. Coins -> *Game Informer* magazines

11

ON SUNDAY, BABA AND I DECIDE TO ACCEPT MR. FARID'S invitation and join some of the mosque members for an afternoon at Kennedy Greenway, a park in central Boston. It's definitely better than sitting at home, waiting for sunset to come so we can eat. Besides, Benj is going to be there, and he'll bring the figurines. If I'm careful to keep it from Baba, I can work a trade into this afternoon.

Baba and I arrive at the State Street T station and follow a line of red brick cutting through the gray pavement. The trail brings us past the deepest parts of the city. When I tilt my head back, the blue skyscrapers seem to brush the scattered clouds above. The roads are all but empty of cars, which seems strange to me, but plenty of people are on foot. Music flits through the air, and street performers play, circled by onlookers. Smells grow stronger—pasta one moment, then burgers, then spices, then coffee. It's so full, so *alive*, that it's almost like I'm in an Istanbul bazaar.

But the nearby food makes my stomach clench, and I can hardly appreciate all the bustling because of my hunger.

"Perhaps we should hurry through," Baba says, a knowing gleam in his eye. "It does not do to linger so near temptation."

I smile and pick up the pace.

Baba doesn't say much as we move past the street performers. I keep glancing at him, trying to read his face. At the sound of music, I feel an ache in my chest, and I'm sure he must feel it, too: the wish for the rebab, and a corner of our own to play on.

We go through a shopping center to another crosswalk. An abandoned carousel is on the far side, with sheets draped over to cover it. A man glides by on a scooter, using a huge plastic bag for a sail. A breeze smelling more of salt than food loosens the tight hunger in my stomach.

Finally, we're in sight of a green park, where families picnic and couples walk their dogs. A group of people from our mosque chat and laugh under the trees. Some teenage boys are kicking around a soccer ball, while elderly men sit on blankets with chess boards. Hamida is bent over a sketch pad. An older boy plays the guitar beside her, and Benj crouches nearby, studying the boy's fingers as he explains chords. Mr. Farid laughs at something the man next to him says, but when he spots us, he waves. Baba lifts his hand, turning toward them.

Beyond the gathering is the Charles River, deep blue under the clear sky, with white boats docked at the wharf.

To me, Baba says in Pashto, "I did not realize it would be so near the water. Will you be all right, Sami?"

"It's fine," I answer, my face heating. The spot is well away from the riverbank. Even though fear churns in my stomach, I know there's no reason to be nervous. Water's always had this effect on me, even before I stepped into the boat that took us from Turkey to Greece. But I don't want to cause a problem. Not when the lines on Baba's face have begun to relax. Not now that he stands straighter and his eyes move quickly to take in the surroundings.

He's not smiling. But it's still something. I don't want to ruin it by drawing attention to the past.

"It's fine," I repeat, a little quieter, as we reach the group.

Mr. Farid rocks to his feet and shakes Baba's hand. "Assalamu alaikum, friend. I'm so glad you have come."

"Walaikum assalam. We are pleased to be here."

While Mr. Farid introduces Baba to his companions, I edge toward Hamida. The boy strumming the guitar must be her brother—they have the same eyes—and his quick song plays along with the shimmering shadows of the leaves. Part of me wants to watch him, to study the chords and see how it's different or similar to the rebab, but it's clear he already has an all-absorbed fan in Benj. Instead, I try to get a look at Hamida's drawing over her shoulder. She's working with a pencil, sketching short, quick lines.

"Hi, Sami," Hamida says, glancing up and covering her sketch with an embarrassed smile.

My neck heats, but I smile back. "Hi."

One of the soccer players calls, "Hey, Omar, come take over for Omid!"

"Sorry, Benj," says Hamida's brother—Omar. He holds out his guitar. "Here, you can practice until I get back."

"Wow, thanks!" Benj settles with the guitar in his lap while Omar goes to join the team. Carefully pressing down on the strings, Benj manages a wobbly chord. He grins at me. "Hey! How's it going?"

"Good." I sit beside him, folding my legs under me.

"I've got the things . . ." Benj looks around and then

drags over a box about the size of my backpack. "Three creepy figurines, as ordered."

I pull the iPod from my backpack and hold it out. "One fixed iPod, as agreed."

We swap, and I can't help smiling wider. Next step: get back to Cobwebs Antiques and sell the figurines.

Hamida leans over to peer at the box. "What's in there?"

"Figurines." I unzip my backpack to squeeze the box inside. "I need to sell them at Cobwebs—I'll probably go tomorrow after school."

"But then you'd miss practice!" Benj protests.

"Yeah, you can't miss! Before you started coming, Layla would always take the game practically by herself." Hamida snaps her fingers. "That's it! Doesn't Layla's mom work at Cobwebs?"

"Yes . . ."

"Layla lives near you, Hamida—I mean, I'm pretty sure." Benj frowns, thinking. "Do you have her number? I have it—in my phone—somewhere—" He swivels around, keeping the guitar on his lap while he pats the ground nearby.

Hamida tilts her head. "No, I don't . . . But if I did, I could just take them over this afternoon. Then no one has to miss practice!"

And, I realize, I won't have to hide the box from Baba. "I have her number," I volunteer. "My phone's right here. I could . . . ask for her address?"

"Good idea!" Hamida says.

I type out a message while Benj finds his phone (he was sitting on it) and Hamida sketches a bit more. After I send the message, I find myself watching her work. She keeps looking from her page to the harbor and back again. My stomach gets a weird knotted feeling, and suddenly I'm not so interested in her drawing anymore.

I turn my attention back to my phone at the same time that Layla's reply pops up on the screen.

"Layla's in if we can work out how to get the figurines to her. Here's her address," I say, and read it out loud.

Hamida starts nodding before I'm even done. "Yep, I live right down the street! Cool! So, I'll take the box to Layla after the picnic."

"Are you sure?" I make myself look her in the face. I want to be absolutely positive she doesn't mind. "I don't want to inconvenience you . . ."

She waves off my concern. "Nah, it's fine. I've never been to her house before—I can't believe she lives so close!"

"It would be an enormous favor, Hamida."

Hamida pulls the box out of my backpack and sets it

next to her. "Don't even worry about it. Now, Benj—have you figured out 'Twinkle, Twinkle, Little Star' yet?"

"Pfft, I'm a pro at that!" Benj starts playing a tune in stumbling strums. Omar, running past us with the game, gives him a thumbs-up.

Hamida sets aside her sketch and leans over to correct Benj's position. I glance down at the open page—a near-perfect copy of our harbor view. I look at the docks to compare it with her drawing. But almost immediately my stomach begins to tighten, like I'm a string on a kite and someone's winding me around the spool. Hamida and Benj's conversation ebbs into a murmur. Excusing myself, I grab my backpack and sit down beside Baba, who's taking a rest at the fringe of the men's circle. Baba's gaze catches on my bag, and he frowns at the empty zipper where my key chain used to hang.

"What happened to your Manchester United key chain?" he asks in quiet Pashto.

"Oh," I stammer. "I—lost it."

"Sami . . ." Baba sounds annoyed. "You know that was important. You are not so careless."

I shrug and loop my arms around my knees and try not to feel like the ground's sinking away from me.

Baba shakes his head slightly and turns to face the boats.

A flash draws my attention to the harbor. The ferry boat backs away from the dock, and the windows blink again with the sun's reflection. People move around on the top deck, exposed to the open air.

Even though the day's warm, my skin goes all sweaty and cold.

In my head, I'm on the plastic boat during our crossing three years ago. The sea tosses us up and down, up and down. Salt coats my skin and clothes and hair and mouth. We have no drinking water. There is water in every direction, but we have no water. Time has lengthened beyond measuring—I am too sick to think of it. There is only the rise and fall, rise and fall, and the whimpers of a child smaller than me and the occasional murmur of men. I have stopped asking Baba how far it is or when we will arrive.

"Sami." Baba nudges my shoulder.

I look up at him, but my mouth is too dry for talk.

"Sami," Baba says again. Baba is here, beside me, in Boston, on dry ground. He is not the Baba who stares out across the water, searching for land that never seems to come. "Sami, get up and walk around. We'll go home, away from the river."

The green grass feels like it's rising and falling, rising and falling, but I climb to my feet. Sluggish and unsteady, I pace slowly while Baba rises. My face burns, but none of the others seem to notice. Baba takes my backpack, makes our excuses to Mr. Farid and the others, and starts walking me down the path toward the street. Before I turn, Hamida points to the box and gives me a thumbs-up. I can't make my mouth smile back, but I nod to her.

As we walk back to the T stop, the wind pricks the sweat on my arms. My thoughts drag in my head, slurring one into the next.

I try to focus on when we finally saw land, and the strangers who rushed to pull the boat to the shallows, and the blankets they wrapped around us, and the priest who gave us scraps of carpet to kneel on as we prayed our gratitude.

But thinking of landing makes me remember the two people in the boat who did not move. How others dragged their bodies onto the sand.

With an effort, I force myself to look around. A mother with a stroller jogs past. Some young men play catch. Kids chase pigeons. Baba's hand rests on my shoulder, and he rubs his thumb back and forth, back and forth. This is the world I live in now. This isn't the Mediterranean Sea. The ferry boat in the harbor is well equipped. No one is in danger.

As the memory passes, I feel foolish. "Sorry," I mutter to Baba.

"No," Baba says, firm but quiet. "It is the way that it is. I know this. Khuday Pak mehriban dey."

God is kind. I lean my head against his arm and close my eyes tightly.

TRADE LOG

Days: 23

THINGS TO TRADE:

Game Informer magazines (Dan)

PLANNED TRADES:

Figurines for money

COMPLETED TRADES:

1. Manchester United key chain -> iPod
2. Coins -> *Game Informer* magazines
3. iPod -> Figurines

12

THREE DAYS LATER, I'M SITTING IN THE SCHOOL cafeteria at the Murder Corner (that's what Dan calls it) under the water stain. The room smells strongly of greasy cheese and overcooked vegetables. Even though I'm here every day, it still takes effort to think around the sounds of plastic trays banging and students talking. Last week, Mrs. Mulligan said she could make arrangements for me to stay on the playground or in the library instead of being in here, but I don't want to create a fuss. Besides, Dan sits with me now during the lunch period.

Dan returns, carrying his tray piled with pasta in a thick yellow sauce (evidently a school favorite—I'm curious to try it after Ramadan), a carton of milk, and a small ice cream. He dumps his backpack on the floor, sits across from me, and tears open the ice cream first. "I brought my dad's old combat boots for our trade. Mom said that I should get rid of them."

"You sure he won't mind?" It seems strange to me that anyone would want to give up a pair of good combat boots. Those shoes can last years if they're treated well. My plar was always proud of his.

"He doesn't care." Dan rolls his eyes and rubs his sleeve against his nose.

"All right . . ." I pull my legs up on the bench and tuck my feet under my thighs. "I have the *Game Informer* magazines. We'll swap at practice."

"Cool. Any news from Layla about the figurines?"

"Yes." The table next to ours breaks into crazy laughter, and I have to lift my voice to a shout. "Layla said Mr. Byrne gave her fifty dollars for the fisher boy, forty-five for the kids holding hands, and fifty for the shepherdess."

"*Nice!*" Dan lifts his hand for a high five.

I hesitate, then half stand so I can reach across the table to lightly smack his palm. As I sit again, I can't help feeling a bit pleased. My third trade—iPod for figurines—and fourth trade—selling them to Cobwebs—are done. We're nine days into Ramadan, and right now I feel more clearheaded than hungry. Baba brings home plenty of nice food from the restaurant, so we have enough to eat in the evenings. I have to stay up later than normal for iftar and tarawih prayers, which means I'm more tired during class, but I'm doing okay. Baba is still quieter than he used to be, but he doesn't seem to be much worse, so if all goes according to plan, he'll be back to normal after Ramadan when I give him the rebab. For once, everything feels like it's falling into place.

Between bites, Dan asks about our game plan for the soccer match this afternoon. We brainstorm ideas—me drawing diagrams in my notebook—until the first bell goes off with a loud *bbbbrrring*. Students burst into action, and the cafeteria volume lifts another notch. Two teachers start giving orders.

"Be right back," Dan says, taking his leftovers and hurrying to the washer lady. While he is fighting his way to the window where they return their trays, I stand and tug on my backpack, thinking, as always, about my trades. I tap open my note app and look through them again. Layla will be bringing the money from Mr. Byrne to practice. I'll have to hide it from Baba—maybe under my mattress? And I'll have the boots from Dan—I could stash them under my clothes in the closet to keep them a secret.

Someone separates from the mob by the door. It's Peter, coming toward me. My stomach sinks, and I glance around for Dan, wanting to leave. He's passing his tray to the lunch lady now. It would be rude to go without him, but Peter's getting closer.

"How'd you like that iPod, *Samantha*?" Peter calls. He's carrying his backpack by the strap, and he flicks my Man United key chain with his other hand.

I keep my mouth shut. Teachers say if you let people like Peter speak their minds, they'll leave you alone. That isn't how it worked in Turkey or Afghanistan, but maybe it will work in America. If I ignore him, Peter might just move on.

I can't help glancing at the key chain again. Baba's eyes were so sad when I told him I'd lost it. If the money weren't for the rebab, it would not have been worth the cost.

"What? You not talking to me anymore?"

I stare past him, wearing the blank expression I used during the smuggling and border crossing. Peter's between me and the door. I have no exit. My neck starts to sweat, but I concentrate on staying mute.

"I just want to know, what have you been listening to on the iPod? The audio is *great*, right?"

His taunting voice begs me to react. He wants to crow. If I agree that the iPod worked, he bullied me and he wins. If I say that the iPod didn't work, he tricked me and he wins. If I do nothing, maybe he'll find someone else to goad. I won't look at him.

Dan hurries over, grabbing his backpack from the table without a glance at Peter. "Come on, Sami. We're going to be late."

"Your best bud was just about to tell me about his favorite bands," Peter says, turning his attention to Dan. He flicks the key chain again. "Assuming they *have* bands in whatever desert he crawled from."

"Back off, Pete."

"I'm just trying to have a conversation! Why did you even pick this guy for the team?"

The team. Even though Dan told Peter I'm not a replacement, Peter's angry that I took what he sees as his spot.

Peter pokes me in the chest. I let him. "Is there an on switch somewhere?"

Dan smacks Peter's hand down. "I said back *off.*"

The air has tightened, an explosion ready to happen. Other kids separate from the crush by the door to come our way. They look curious, excited—spectators hoping for a scene. If Dan doesn't cool off, we're all going to get in trouble. My mor used to say, *Once you lose your head, you've lost the battle.*

"Dan, stop," I murmur under my breath.

"What are you so wound up about, Danny Boy?" Peter goads. "You're both such retards. An iPod for a key chain? You were totally asking for it!"

"You're a flipping jerk!" Dan jabs a finger at Peter. "But guess what, loser?"

I sense what Dan's about to say. I try to cut in. "Dan—"

"I fixed the iPod, and Sami just made over a hundred dollars off it." Dan crosses his arms and grins. "So who's the real idiot?"

Frustration crackles through my chest. *"Dan."*

"What?" Peter scowls. "You did *what*?" His eyes turn back toward me.

About ten kids have gathered in a semicircle now, trapping us in the corner, Dan and me with our backs against the wall. They jostle each other, and Peter notices his audience.

"What's happening over there?" Mrs. Mulligan calls, spying our huddle. She shoos the last of the other students out. "Time to go to class!"

"You're a dirty cheat!" Peter shoves me so hard I stumble. "If the iPod works, I want it back. That's not a fair trade!"

Dan pushes Peter away. "He can't get it back, bacon brain."

"Then give me the money," Peter demands, looking straight at me instead of Dan.

I shake my head.

He leans in. "You wanna know what we do to people like you, bomb lover?"

Bomb lover. A loud rush swells in my ears.

Glass shattering across the yard, Baba's face as he reaches for me, a hollow roar that freezes me in place, and my plar—my mor—

"Shut up!" Dan snaps.

"What's going on?" Mrs. Mulligan says, making a gap in the kids.

I shrink back from her, from them all. My throat has gone drier than dust.

"We'll see who's the idiot," Peter hisses at Dan. His eyes flick to me. "You don't belong here, terrorist."

"The Taliban have claimed the attack," the Afghan policeman says. Baba's fingers dig into my shoulder . . .

Peter raises his voice. "Give me my iPod!"

"Hey, everyone, calm down." Mrs. Mulligan steps between us. She's wide enough that Peter has to retreat. "What's this about? Why aren't you all in class?"

Some of the watching kids sneak away. It takes concentration for me to focus on what's being said. My skin turns prickly and cold, and I rub the scar on my arm again and again.

"He stole my iPod," Peter says, nodding toward me. "He *stole* it and won't give it back."

"You're a filthy liar!" Dan shouts.

"Calm down, Dan," Mrs. Mulligan scolds. "Everyone, take a deep breath."

She waits, hands on hips, for a few seconds. I try to breathe, but it's hard. Is being accused of stealing enough to get me deported to Turkey—or even Afghanistan?

Mrs. Mulligan inhales and exhales loudly. "So he stole it, did he, Peter?"

"I *saw* him going through my backpack last Thursday. I just didn't realize he'd taken it until today."

"Is that so?" Mrs. Mulligan lifts an eyebrow at him. "Peter, do you know where I was sitting on Thursday?"

"Uh . . ."

"Right where I always do. There." She points to a nearby table, the one that gives a good view of the whole room. "I saw you hand over an iPod."

"Uh . . ."

"Ha!" shouts Dan, triumphant.

My heart gives a feeble beat.

"*However*"—Mrs. Mulligan shoots Dan a look—"you *all* have created a significant disruption. We need to talk to Principal Myers about this."

"But—" Dan protests.

"That's not—" starts Peter at the same time.

"No complaining. Come on." Mrs. Mulligan points us out the door.

As he falls into step beside me, Peter leans over to whisper, "Who do you think they're gonna believe caused this—me or ISIS Junior?"

When he straightens, he's already smiling.

TRADE LOG

Days: 20

Have: $145

Need: $555

PLANNED TRADES:

Game Informer magazines for combat boots (Dan)

COMPLETED TRADES:

1. Manchester United key chain -> iPod
2. Coins -> *Game Informer* magazines
3. iPod -> Figurines
4. Figurines -> $145

13

THE THREE OF US ARE KEPT WAITING OUTSIDE THE principal's office. We already talked to him once, but we had to go to afternoon classes. Now we've been brought here again. I hold my backpack in my lap and fix my gaze on the clock: 3:10. School is ending now, and our parents are supposed to come get us.

Which, for me, means Baba.

I start counting the tiles on the floor of the waiting area, again. When my head fills with numbers, it's easier to avoid memories.

The school phoned Baba. I tried to convince them not to—I didn't want Baba to take any time off, not when he'd have to make it up later. If I had the money on me, I almost would have given it to Peter just to make him stop all this, to keep Baba from getting involved.

But a hard stubbornness has settled in my stomach, and it keeps me silent.

Because he's wrong.

Bomb lover keeps going through my head. *Terrorist.*

I pinch my wrist and concentrate on the tiles. *Twenty-three, twenty-four . . .* Just keep counting. Think about anything other than a past full of bombs and a future full of jail. Or a future deported. I'm not sure which is worse.

The bell rings and I start, nearly dropping my bag. In the main hall, voices shout and sneakers squeak and lockers slam. I lean my head on the wall. This is so far from the day I'd expected—going to the rec center, playing soccer, trading with Dan.

Dan's sitting a few chairs over, sketching soccer-maneuver plans in his notebook. If he had held his temper, this wouldn't have happened. I know he was just trying to help, but I feel annoyed anyway. Dan's defense has only made me a bigger target for Peter. And Dan hasn't shown the least sign of being aware that he made things worse.

The door to the office drags on the floor as Baba pushes it open. I sit up straight. He shoots me a confused, worried look but says to the secretary, "I am Sami's grandfather. I was told to come meet the principal?"

The secretary nods. "Just have a seat for now. We're still waiting on Dan's and Peter's parents to arrive."

"Thank you." Baba takes the chair next to mine.

I hug my backpack tighter, not sure what to say to him. Peter steals sideways glances at us, especially at Baba's wiry beard and his gray lungee in its simple twist. Anger coils around my lungs, but I hold it in.

Baba doesn't say anything, either. He is tired—I can tell by the way he lays his palms flat against his knees. I feel his uncertainty as he slowly examines the room— the tiled floor and water-stained ceiling, the secretary's desk and old computer, the filing cabinet behind her, and the stuffed cat lying on top of it. This is the first time he's been called to a principal's office. I've never been in trouble, not even in the makeshift schools in Greece and Turkey.

The clock on the wall ticks slowly to three thirty. Most of the noise in the school dies down as people leave, and then the only sound is the secretary scrolling through her Facebook page. Though she's made the window small on her computer to hide what she's doing, I can still see the white-and-blue layout from where I'm sitting. Sometimes she snorts at a funny post. Peter watches the door, switching between hooking his feet around the legs of his chair and letting them swing free. Dan doesn't look up from his soccer schemes. I'm beginning to wonder if he actually cares about anything but them.

At 3:35 a woman hurries in, pushing the door so hard it hits the wall. She's dressed in a wrinkled suit, her hair pulled back but falling out of the tie. She's on the phone and says quickly, "I know, but I'll be there as soon as I can. I'm sorry. See you then."

When she puts the phone into her purse, she accidentally drops her CharlieCard on the floor. It lands near Baba's feet, and he picks it up before she can finish her tight sigh.

"Oh, thanks," she says, accepting it and pushing her hair back. Taking a deep breath, she closes her eyes a moment and then turns to Peter. Her eyebrows lift a little in worry. She sits, touching Peter's arm. "How are you doing, kid?"

He pulls away, rolling his eyes.

"Hi, Susan," she says to the secretary.

"Hi, Katrina. How's the dog?"

"Doing better, thanks."

The door opens again, and this time a woman with Dan's same blond hair slips in, her cheeks—already red—getting even darker when she glances around the room. "Sorry, everyone, my—uh—Kevin was going to come, but—anyway, sorry I'm late."

"No problem. I'll just get Mr. Myers," the secretary says, opening the principal's door. "They're all here, Jon."

"This is *stupid*," Peter mutters, picking up his backpack from the floor and throwing it onto the chair next to him.

"Shush, Peter," his mom murmurs.

Dan's mom sits, glancing from Dan—busy with his soccer sketches—to me. "Are you Sami? Dan's said a lot about you."

"I, um . . . yes." I glance at Baba.

But he's staring at Peter's backpack. My Manchester United key chain is right there, clear for anyone to see. My heart suddenly feels like it's been sucked into quicksand.

Mr. Myers comes out. He's a gray-haired man with a thick mustache, a bit like the US president Theodore Roosevelt we've studied in class.

"Hello, Ms. Cooper, Ms. Reeves, Mr. Safi." He shakes hands with each of them. "So we had a bit of a disturbance today. Started over an argument. Daniel Reeves says Sami traded a key chain for an iPod."

Baba looks at me slowly. "Sami?"

I open and close my mouth.

"Peter agreed to the trade because the iPod was broken. Then Dan fixed it, and Peter wanted it back. At any rate, the argument escalated, which is why we're all here."

"I'm so sorry," Dan's mom says. "But I—I have an appointment with my lawyer in just over an hour, and I need to get across town. I really hate to do this, but could you just let us know what the kids are facing?"

Before Mr. Myers answers, Peter's mom leans over to put her hand over Dan's mom's. "It's okay, Meg." She looks at Baba and the principal. "Can we call this whole thing end-of-the-year tension and leave it there? I'm not upset with Dan or this boy—Sami?—and from what you said they didn't do anything strictly against school policy . . ."

"Actually, some of Peter's statements would qualify as hate speech under our policy."

Dan glares at Peter. "He called Sami a terrorist and a bomb lover."

Baba's brows lower. I want to disappear.

"What?" says Peter's mom. "Oh my gosh. He shouldn't have said that, but I'm sure he didn't mean it. Did you, Peter?"

Peter's expression turns pleading. "I was only joking."

"He was *not*," Dan growls.

"Daniel." His mom gives him a silencing look.

"I'm sorry." Peter straightens up in his chair and clasps his hands in his lap. He looks directly at me, eyes wide and sincere. "I didn't mean to say that stuff. I thought it would be funny, but it was dumb. I'm really, *really* sorry. Okay?"

They're all watching me now. Mistrust grumbles in my chest, but when I look around the room, it's clear from the faces of Pete's and Dan's moms, and even Mr. Myers, that they want me to agree. And if I don't, then it will only expose my plan—Mr. Myers will want to know what happened to the iPod, and Baba will find out about the trades.

I give a small nod.

"Good." Mr. Myers smiles. "Is everyone okay with that?"

Mrs. Reeves gives a quick glance at the clock on the wall and nods.

Ms. Cooper smiles gratefully. "Yes, I'll talk to Peter more about it at home."

Baba hesitates, but rises stiffly and murmurs, "Very well."

Mr. Myers fixes Peter in a long look. "Peter, I hope you realize now that what you say can have serious consequences, even if you didn't mean it."

Peter lowers his eyes and drops his shoulders. "Yes, sir."

Mr. Myers puts a hand on his office door. "All right, then. I'll see that the issue is settled from our side of things."

"Thank you," Baba says, and Mrs. Reeves and Ms. Cooper echo him. I grab the door and hold it open for everyone. The mothers go out first, talking quietly together.

Dan passes me and whispers, "Don't be too late for practice." Then he sprints in front of the others.

I clench my jaw but don't answer. Of course Dan's only thinking of the game.

As Peter walks out, his foot hits my ankle, and I bite my cheek to keep from gasping. Something tells me that wasn't an accident.

Baba goes last, quiet and thoughtful. We walk together down the now-empty hallway, my hands clenched around my backpack straps.

He doesn't speak until we reach the school parking lot. Then he slowly turns. In Pashto, he says, "You told me you lost the key chain. Why did you lie?"

"I-I did not think it was a big deal." I hate the words as I say them. But if I told him the truth, my plan would fall apart. He wouldn't let me do the trades, and then we might never get the rebab back. "I thought it didn't matter."

He studies me, and it takes all my concentration to keep from squirming. "Do you have the iPod, then?"

I hesitate. "No. I gave it to someone else."

"Sami, what is happening?" His voice softens, like it does when he's worried. "Why are you keeping these things from me?"

"Nothing's happening. It's fine." I stop at the corner. His restaurant is straight ahead, but I need to turn to go to the rec center. "I have to get to practice before it's over."

Baba hesitates but finally puts his hand on my head. "We will talk about this when I get home," he says. Then he goes on down the street.

I keep my eyes fixed on the red hand of the cross-walk sign. I won't tell him the truth until Eid. I just need to come up with a better story.

The lie feels wrong, though—it makes my head itch and my toes curl. I've never had to keep something from Baba before. It makes me feel unclean.

This is all Peter's fault. And Dan's, for giving Peter ammunition, whether intentionally or not. If Dan hadn't told Peter about fixing the iPod, it never would have escalated this far.

The red hand changes to a white walking person.

I'll think about the lie later.

Right now, I need to deal with Dan.

TRADE LOG

Days: 20

Have: $145

Need: $555

PLANNED TRADES:

Game Informer magazines for combat boots (Dan)

COMPLETED TRADES:

1. Manchester United key chain -> iPod
2. Coins -> *Game Informer* magazines
3. iPod -> Figurines
4. Figurines -> $145

14

WHEN I COME INTO THE REC CENTER GYM, COACH IS already running the team through the last half of the game. I hang at the edge, disappointed, though I knew it would be nearly done by now. Dan's already in the action, even though he could only have arrived a few minutes ago.

The door swings shut with a loud bang, and Coach notices me. "Come on, Sami! Benj had to leave early. You can make the teams even. You're on blue today."

I jog over. Dan is on my team, which irritates me. I'm not sure I want to see him at all after he blurted about the iPod to Peter. If he had just kept his head down, none of this would have happened. Baba wouldn't be disappointed in me. Peter wouldn't be dead set on hating me even more. I try to keep my expression neutral as

I pull on the blue mesh over-shirt. Everyone has stopped to wait. With another prick of annoyance, I notice Layla's on red. That does not bode well for our offense.

"All right, everyone, let's kick off again." Coach arranges us. He has to put me on defense because Dan's on offense. I normally don't mind defense, but today I want to grind my teeth in frustration. "Three, two, one—"

Dan kicks off, and the offense runs down the other end of the gym. I move from one foot to the other, watching the ball get passed around on the far side. Dan takes it too close to the goalkeeper, and she grabs it and throws it above their heads.

Layla is on it the moment it hits the floor. I run for her, but she slides around me, and before any of us can do anything, she's shot it into the goal.

The other team shouts in victory.

Dan trots to us, red-faced and scowling. "Jeez, Sami, you've got to stay with her!"

My fists clench, and my face goes hot. "Maybe if you hadn't gone so close to the goal before you were ready to shoot, the ball would still be in their half."

Dan's glare darkens, but Coach claps his hands.

"Return to position! And keep it light!" he calls with a look at us. Great, now Coach is mad at me, too. "Get ready for kickoff."

I retreat to my place on defense, and Dan takes his spot farther up. I try to push the anger away, to concentrate on the game, but mostly I just want to kick the ball into Dan's head.

When the ball comes into my area again, Dan trails the red team kid. I shove myself in the way, steal the ball, and shoot it toward the middle of the court instead of passing to Dan.

"Hey!" he snaps, but doesn't have time to say more before he has to run back down the court.

Soon it's clear we're losing the game. Dan and I keep clashing. I pass the ball too far once, so Dan loses it. I pass it too hard later, so it hits him with a smack in the shins. He elbows me out of the way when he runs past and shoots it over my head twice.

"What's your *problem*?" Dan hisses under his breath while we wait for another kickoff.

"What's *yours*?"

We're so far behind it's hardly worth trying. Layla loses a pass, and the ball skids in my direction. One of the larger red team players sprints right at me. I get the ball out from under my feet and pivot—but my shoe skids on the gym floor and I fall. Pain shoots up my leg, but I hardly notice. The other team steals the ball. Someone grabs my arm and pulls me up. Dan. He doesn't look at me or say anything, though, just jogs after the players, too late to stop them from getting another goal.

Now the other team is one point from a win. There's no way we'll catch up, but Dan goes after the ball anyway. I don't know if he's too stubborn to admit it's a lost cause, or if quitting just isn't in his playbook—on or off the field. Somehow he makes it around their defense and charges straight for the goalie—a girl with wild, kinky hair who's taller than all of us—but she doesn't back down. The trick doesn't work. She grabs the ball and throws.

With a bounce, it lands near me. I get ready to pass it back to an offensive player, but I'm instantly surrounded. I try to keep the ball between my feet, but Layla and the others—it feels like at least twenty kids—keep trying to get around me. The world tightens, full of ankles and elbows and sweat, and I'm entirely cut off from my team.

My lungs shrink.

Cold sweat breaks out across my arms and face.

Then Dan shoves in and kicks the ball away. My frustration starts to flare—but instead of following the ball to try to control it himself, he actually *lets* Layla steal it.

While their team bolts off toward our goal, Dan casts a glance at me. "Okay?"

My chest hurts. And it feels like I haven't breathed in a while. But I nod. "Thanks."

The other team gets the winning point, and Coach calls time. They erupt into celebration. Dan grimaces and shrugs. My anger finally dissolves. And I'm suddenly ashamed of the way the game went.

"Hey," I say, offering my hand to him. "That was a pretty cool chip—would've been a good Panenka, if we were on penalty."

"Yeah." He hesitates, then shakes my hand. "Too bad Julie doesn't budge for anyone."

We stand there in awkward silence while the rest of the team talks about the game.

Dan scratches the back of his head. "Hey, um, sorry about Peter. The guy's a real jerk."

"Yeah." I pause, not sure what else to say. I wasn't really mad at Peter—he acted just how I'd expect. But Dan . . . Dan betrayed my trust. "It's all right. Maybe just . . . don't say so much next time?" It comes out like a question.

Dan groans. "Yeah, I really wish I'd kept my mouth shut. He just makes me so mad!"

It's not an apology, but at least he can admit he made a mistake. "Were you two friends?" I ask.

"Since third grade." Dan frowns. "But not anymore." He shrugs his shoulders and then turns to me with a grin. "You want to do the trade now?"

"All right," I say, even though I'm not sure I'll ever get used to how quickly Dan can change the subject.

I follow Dan across the busy room and open my backpack. The magazines in hand, I rub my thumb along their spines. Dan pulls out his dad's combat boots and tosses them to me. They land with a thud at my feet. They're black with dark buckles and thick straps instead of laces. The grooves on the bottoms are worn down a little, but not bad.

"Those work for you?" Dan asks, rubbing his shoulder and rolling his head. "'Cause I don't want to lug them home."

"Yeah, these are good." I give him the magazines. "So your dad was a tanker?"

"Huh?"

"His boots are tanker boots. That's why they don't have laces."

"Oh." Dan flips through the glossy pages. "Yeah, I guess."

He doesn't look at me, and a silence stretches between us. I examine the boots. They might still be touched with a bit of Kabul mud or Kandahar dust. While he was away from Dan, he was walking in my land. Fighting in my land.

My stomach feels like it's being stretched, pulled farther and farther from me. His dad and my plar fought on the same side. If they were stationed in the same battalion, they might have even given their lives for each other.

I glance over at Dan. Even though he made a huge mess of everything today, I think he is my ally. But I'm still not totally sure he's my friend.

TRADE LOG

Days: 20

Have: $145

Need: $555

THINGS TO TRADE:

Combat boots

COMPLETED TRADES:

1. Manchester United key chain -> iPod
2. Coins -> *Game Informer* magazines
3. iPod -> Figurines
4. Figurines -> $145
5. Magazines -> Combat boots

15

"HEY, DID YOU JUST DO A TRADE?" LAYLA ASKS FROM behind me.

I jump, surprised. Dan seems startled, too.

"You guys okay?" She looks between us.

"Yeah," I answer. Dan nods. "We're fine. Just traded the *Game Informer* magazines for combat boots."

"Nice! And I have the money from Cobwebs." Layla digs an envelope out of her backpack and passes it to me. "What are all these trades *for*, anyway?"

"I've been wondering the same thing," Coach says, walking over.

Dan glances up, his mouth open to answer for me. But he hesitates. Closes his mouth. Turns to me. "You should tell them."

My head screams that telling more people is

dangerous. That the more people know, the more opportunities there are for something to go wrong. But Layla and Coach are already involved—Layla helped me do the trade with Cobwebs, and Coach gave me the magazines. And I don't think they're like Peter. I don't believe they'll use the truth to hurt me.

And suddenly I have the urge to tell them everything, as if my honesty now will help the lie to Baba be less of a stain.

Bending my head, I say in the direction of the combat boots, "My baba—grandfather—had a rebab. It's an Afghan instrument. He used to be a professional player, with concerts and everything. When we left Afghanistan, he carried it with him during our journey—it was one of the only things we brought. But about two weeks ago, I was playing it in a T station, and someone stole it from me. I found it in a music shop in the city, but the man won't give it to me unless I pay seven hundred dollars. I don't have any money, so I'm trying to get seven hundred dollars with trades."

Coach frowns, but one of the other kids calls a question to him. He moves off to answer.

"Oh, wow." Layla makes a face and tugs a braid. "Crazy! How could someone just take something like that?"

"Right?" Dan chimes in. "And the shop guy is a real sleaze to not give it back."

Layla's phone buzzes, and she checks her messages. "I've got to go. But my mom says there's an estate sale on Saturday. Do you guys want to join in? Could be a good place to find more stuff to trade."

"Poke around someone else's stuff? Definitely!" Dan grins. "I'll ask the Parent."

I hesitate. Saturday is the only day Baba has off this week. I can't pass up the opportunity to purchase more items to trade, but I don't like to think of him sitting alone in the apartment.

Layla nudges my shoulder. "Your grandpa could come, too, if he wants."

"That might work," I agree. Maybe a day out would lift his spirits.

"Great. Text me your addresses and we can pick you up on our way. I'm excited! I need to find a birthday present for my mom—" Her phone buzzes again, and Layla hurries toward the gym door. "Got to run! See you then!"

Dan puts the magazines carefully in his backpack. "Julie wants those combat boots—I bet you anything. Even if they don't fit, she'd trade her right arm for them."

"Julie?" I glance toward our teammates. Only a few are lingering to talk.

"She was the keeper on the other team today."

I spot her. She's wearing a T-shirt a few sizes too big and has her curly hair pulled back in a bushy ponytail. "Why would she want your dad's combat boots?"

"She plans to join the army, first chance she gets." Dan rocks to his feet. "I told her I'd bring 'em by, so I think she's brought some pictures of stuff for you to look at. I've got to get home—Mom will freak if she gets back from lawyer-talk and the house is a mess. See you tomorrow?"

"Sure."

While Dan leaves, I tie the boots' straps together. They definitely *smell* like they were in combat—rank with old sweat. Hopefully Julie won't mind.

"Sami?" Coach comes up beside me.

"Yes, sir?"

"I had an idea—it might help you get some extra money. I have a friend at Northeastern University who is working on his PhD. His dissertation is about the migrant crisis—I mean, that's part of it—and he's trying to collect firsthand stories from people who have made it to the US. I'm pretty sure he has some funds to compensate you for your time."

It's a bit difficult to understand him—there are a lot of words and I'm not totally sure of their meaning. "What would I have to do?"

"Just meet with him, talk about why you left Afghanistan, and what happened between then and now." Coach fishes in his pocket and pulls out a business card. "Here, this is his information."

I take the card. It's just like the one we used to fix the iPod. My thumb leaves a dirty smudge on the white paper. Coach's friend's name is printed in bold, black letters, LINCOLN TRUDEAU, with his number and email address below. There's another line I didn't notice before:

PhD Candidate, Northeastern University—Communities Re-Formed on These Shores: An Examination of Historical and Recent Migration to the Eastern US Through the Lens of Cultural History, Adaptation, and Society.

"He's a great guy," Coach says. "I'm sure he'd love to talk with you."

"Thanks," I say, but I doubt I'll contact him. I try not to remember what happened to my home, so why would I talk about it with a stranger? The trades are going well— it's nice of Coach to come up with a way for me to make more money, but I don't need it. "I will think about it."

"I understand. You have a printer at home?"

I shake my head.

"No problem. I'll ask Juniper to print off the permission slip, just in case you decide to talk with Lincoln. Actually—have we had your grandfather sign the forms for the rec center yet?"

I shake my head again. "I was going to make sure Baba does tonight. But I do have those forms."

"Okay, definitely bring them on Monday." He pauses. But he just flashes a smile at me. "See you tomorrow."

"See you." I go back to tying the boot straps together, and once I'm sure my knot will hold, I swing my backpack on one shoulder and the boots on the other. I look for Julie and spot her across the room, already staring at the boots.

I take a deep breath and walk toward her. But when I get there, before I have a chance to say anything, she asks bluntly, "Dan said you might trade those?" She immediately pulls out her phone. "He told me to bring pictures for you. Here, have a look."

I lean over her shoulder while she scrolls, tucking the business card into my back pocket. Julie has an old winter coat, some DVDs, German shepherd stuffed animals. None of it gives me any real ideas. Where would I trade them next?

A medium-sized bin of something that looks like markers pops up on her phone.

"Hold on." I stop her before she flies past. "What's this?"

"Bin from art camp. My mom made me go last year." Julie taps the photo to make it bigger. "There's a ton of stuff in here. Some Spectrum Noir markers, a sketchbook, colored pencils, watercolors . . ."

Hamida draws. She can do so much with just a pencil—and she told Mr. Farid she wanted real supplies! My heart pounds, and I start to grin. "I'll trade you for the supplies."

"You got it, trade boy. I'll even dig through my things and see if I can find any more art stuff to throw in."

"Great." This is perfect—better than I could have asked for. "I'll hold the boots, and we can trade at practice?"

"You got it." She gives me a thumbs-up and then follows her friend out.

I trail behind, pleased. But as I'm walking through the main lobby, Miss Juniper waves me over.

"Hey, Sami, here are the forms," she says, passing them to me. "Two for the rec center, in case you need extra, and one for Lincoln Trudeau, if you decide to talk to him."

Unease pricks up my back. I take the forms slowly. "Thanks."

Coach stands by the desk, watching. "You know, Sami—" he starts, then hesitates before he goes on, "This doesn't have to be just for the money—sometimes it's good to talk to someone. My parents came over from Somalia. I think, maybe if they had talked more . . ." He sighs. "But maybe they couldn't. I don't know. It's worth a try, though, right?"

Somalia. That's where his accent is from. Miss Juniper gives Coach a sad smile. I murmur thanks again, and slip out the door.

I have plenty of leads on trades. Coach might think talking is good, and Mrs. Michele might think memories shouldn't be locked away. But I can handle this on my own.

Talking is the last thing I want to do.

TRADE LOG

Days: 20

Have: $145

Need: $555

PLANNED TRADES:

Combat boots for art supplies (Julie)

COMPLETED TRADES:

1. Manchester United key chain -> iPod
2. Coins -> *Game Informer* magazines
3. iPod -> Figurines
4. Figurines -> $145
5. Magazines -> Combat boots

16

ON SATURDAY MORNING, BABA AND I WAIT OUTSIDE THE apartment for our ride. I have put all of my earnings in a plastic bag, which I'm keeping in my pocket. Hopefully there will be something at the sale I can buy—something that will lead to more trades.

"So, Dan is the one who normally plays defense on your team." Baba adjusts his white taqiyah on his head. He doesn't mention the principal's office. "Layla is the girl who does offense. Mrs. Michele is her mother."

"Right." Baba has been practicing their names and his English since we woke before dawn. I think he wants to be sure not to embarrass me.

Baba nods. "I think I can remember these."

A blue minivan rounds the corner, Mrs. Michele at the wheel. I wave.

As soon as the car rolls to a stop, Layla bounds out of the passenger seat, calling, "Your grandpa can sit with my mom in the front!"

She throws open the sliding door and dives into the back before I can stop her. Baba looks a bit uncomfortable, glancing uncertainly at the empty passenger seat beside Mrs. Michele. In Kandahar, he would never sit in the front with a woman unless she was his wife or daughter.

"It's normal for men and women here," I remind him in Pashto. "It's a different world, remember?"

He gives me a sly glance.

Mrs. Michele rolls down her window. "Come on in! We're not *too* scary."

Baba walks around to the front passenger side. Behind him there are two seats in the middle, with a toddler in his car seat leaving only one empty. Layla motions me to the back, where she's sitting beside Dan.

"Hi," I say, taking the spot on the other side of Layla. Raising my voice a little, I add, "Baba, this is Dan and Layla. Dan, Layla, this is my grandfather, Habibullah Safi."

"Hi!" Layla waves.

"Good to meet you, sir," Dan says, suddenly formal. "I mean—officially."

"And you, Dan." Baba turns in his seat and nods to him. "Hello, Layla."

Mrs. Michele points to the toddler. "Mr. Safi, Sami, this is my youngest—Jared. Micah and Alex are Layla's other brothers."

"But Alex wanted to sleep in." Layla shakes her head, disgusted. "And Dad and Micah are visiting colleges."

"Hello, Jared," Baba says, giving a little wave. Jared grins at him. Mrs. Michele starts off as soon as we're buckled.

"So, how're you doing?" asks Dan.

"Good," I answer, then hesitate. "Your parents didn't want to go to the sale?"

"Yeah, the Parent"—he says it like a title or a name—"had to work. But she didn't care if I came, so here I am."

"Oh." It clicks suddenly, and I feel stupid for not realizing sooner. *The* parent. That nickname wasn't just Dan being odd. It was because he only has one—his mother. What happened to his father? And why did Dan have his boots?

I'm not sure how to ask, and it probably isn't my place anyway. Dan doesn't seem fazed by my question. He's looking out the window, pointing out landmarks to me and Layla, so I let the subject drop.

Classical music drifts over the radio, and the car

smells faintly of hot plastic and crackers. The drive across the city passes with murmurs from the front of Baba's conversation with Mrs. Michele and Dan launching into funny stories. Layla perches on the edge of the seat, straining against her seat belt, watching the road for any sign of something called "punch buggies." I look out my window as the cramped apartment complexes change to concrete highway. When we cross the Charles River, I turn my gaze to the floor. The distance between Baba and me seems to stretch. I wish I were next to him. Without his arm around my shoulder, the concrete bridge quivers beneath the wheels, the height grows until the air gets thin, the seconds slow to minutes and minutes to hours—I clench my hands in my lap and don't breathe until we reach the far side.

We pull off at Winthrop and wind down quiet back-streets, past houses that might as well be mansions.

"That's mine!" Layla exclaims suddenly, pointing at a green one. "Mom! Mom! I claim that one!"

I glance at her, surprised. If she lives somewhere like this, why does she come all the way to the rec center?

But then her mother points to a blue one and says, "Well, that one's *mine*."

"Oooh, I like the porch." Layla nods her approval. She pokes me. "Which do you want?"

"Um." They're all so big and grand and *different* from anything I've known. Suddenly I'm thinking of the single-story house in Kandahar, with its white walls and pink bougainvillea and my mor jani's voice drifting from inside.

I want that home with an ache that steals my breath and burns my eyes.

Trying to hide it from Layla, I point blindly. "That one."

"Good choice! Sweet garden out front."

"I'll take the red one," Dan volunteers.

Mrs. Michele turns the corner onto another, smaller street packed with cars.

"And here we are," she says cheerfully, unbuckling her seat belt.

Dan and Layla clamber out, and I follow more slowly. They're eager to gawk at the house, but I go around to help Baba rise from his seat. He accepts my arm with a grimace. In Pashto, he says, "These old bones don't want to cooperate today, it seems."

"Just move slowly." I adjust my grip so I can hold him better. "Be careful."

Baba gains his feet and ruffles my hair. "I am fine."

Dan comes bounding back to us. "Well, are we going to raid this mansion or not?"

"Those were *exactly* my thoughts, Dan," Mrs. Michele chimes in. She picks up Jared, pushes the car door shut, and lifts him onto her shoulders. "Here we go!"

Mrs. Michele leads us around the crowd of parked cars to a house near the end of the street. It's three stories high, painted white with a green roof. Mr. Byrne is visiting on the front porch and greets Mrs. Michele as we approach.

While the adults talk, Jared reaches for Baba. Baba leans forward to tease Jared with his finger. He used to do that with the refugee children along the route—he could always get the most irritable child to laugh. Soon Jared's grinning.

Layla elbows me. "Come on. Let's go!"

"Do you mind if we explore on our own?" I ask Baba in quick Pashto.

"No," he answers. His eyes have brightened, and Jared catches his finger while he is distracted. "Go on. Be careful."

Layla slips inside, Dan and me on her heels. Immediately, one thing becomes clear: The old owner really, *really* loved ducks.

There are duck paintings, duck statues, duck toys. Wooden ducks, clay ducks, glass ducks. The hallway has already been pretty picked over, but the living room is covered in them.

"Wow," Dan whispers. "It's like a duck graveyard or something."

"Duck mania," Layla adds. She points to some of the painted wooden ducks. "You'd be surprised, though—*plenty* of collectors love this sort of stuff. Duck decoys are especially popular."

"Duck decoys?" I ask.

"Hunters use them, I think. Mostly people like to display the antique ones." She moves around the old couch and table. "How much do you have to spend, Sami?"

"I brought a hundred and forty-five dollars." I hope I won't have to use it all today, but I can if we find something really, really good.

"Cool. Let's hunt treasure!"

"There are *twenty* ducks in this room," Dan says, "in case anyone was curious."

We comb through the living room and head into the kitchen. I can't help feeling a bit like a looter, rifling through the belongings of whoever used to live here. A strange, sad smell lingers around everything—a blend of newspaper and dust. But I also can't help being fascinated. It's a life I'll probably never have, one filled with huge hallways and too much stuff. And ducks. One hundred and twelve by the third room, according to Dan's count.

The house is built right on the beach, which Dan and Layla love—they keep stopping by the windows to gawk at the distant city skyline. I stay in the center of the room, but I can't help catching glimpses of the water. Though it's a cloudy day, some boats bob out there, and they make my fingers shake. I focus harder on examining the things I might buy.

There are age-darkened paintings, piles of tangled jewelry, and ancient books with leather covers so soft they feel like skin. The crowded assortment makes me think of the market in Kandahar. Sometimes my mor would take me to the women's bazaar on the days my plar or Baba could not make it to the one for men. She tried to go as seldom as possible, because of the attacks. They happened often, and at random, wherever people were gathered. Going to school put me at risk. Going to the bazaar just asked for trouble.

But she took me sometimes. She would lift her chadari off the hook by the door. It was always pale blue, the most common color since the Taliban came (before I was born). She never followed the trendy dyes the fashionable women wore—pink, green, or gold. All those hues stood out in the sea of blue. My mor wanted to be unseen, unidentifiable.

She would grin at me before she fastened the chadari

to the top of her head, letting the flowy fabric cover her body and adjusting the rectangular mesh so it rested over her eyes.

"Now I am invisible," she would say.

"Yes," I would answer, putting on my shoes.

She would place her hands on her hips, making the chadari spread like a parachute. "Will you find me? Take a look at my shalwar kameez and sandals. What am I wearing?"

I would study her, though I never remembered what she wore the second we were separated. Details about clothes always slid right out of my head.

But I didn't need her shoes or trousers to recognize her. I knew her in the way she walked, the way her hands would flit free of the chadari as she moved, like she wanted to relish the air. I knew her in a crowd; in night or day, I knew her. She was my mor jani. Of course I knew her.

Would I still know her now?

"Sami?" Layla waves her hand in front of my face, and the image of my mor fades back to the place I cannot reach. "You ready to go to the next room?"

I swallow and nod, following. Dan has already disappeared inside.

"Two hundred and fifty-four, two hundred and fifty-five . . . ," he mutters, still counting ducks.

This is one of the last rooms. It must have been an office, because there's a massive old desk. On the desk is a laptop. I walk over, curious. So far it's the only thing that looks kind of new in the entire house.

"What do you guys think of this?" I ask, drawing their attention from the bookshelves and ducks.

"Oh!" Layla exclaims, hurrying over.

"Hold on—let me see." Dan leaves his duck count to push the laptop's on button. "You can't just buy any old computer. It could be crawling with viruses or cat pictures. Or the RAM could be trashed. Let me do a quick check."

"Okay," Layla says, "but if there *are* cat pictures, leave them. Someone might trade extra for that."

Dan grunts and clicks through the opening screen.

"How much is it?" Layla leans around him to look. "Sami, can you find the price?"

I think I saw a tag on the top before Dan opened it, so I wedge myself between the desk edge and the wall to get a better angle. "There's a sticker here. It's one hundred dollars."

"That's great!" Layla says. "I bet you could resell it for double!"

My stomach squirms, though, somewhere between excitement and dread. One hundred dollars will be almost all I have. Worth it, maybe—but still a risk.

"First you should let me run some more tests," Dan says, not lifting his gaze from the screen. "They've wiped the hard drive, so no cat pictures or anything else, which is good."

"Well, the cat pictures would have been nice," Layla chips in.

I squeeze out from behind the desk, but as I do, my arm knocks the plug. It falls free of the laptop, and the computer immediately shuts off.

"What happened?" Dan asks, startled.

Frowning, I put the plug in again. The computer starts when Dan presses the power button. "The battery must be broken," I say, discouraged.

Dan fishes out his phone. "You could buy a new one." To Layla, he says, "I'll check eBay, you get Amazon."

"Aye, aye!" Layla grabs her phone, too, and starts typing.

I wait, chewing my lip and wishing I had data on my phone. When they ask for the laptop model, I read off the name. I wait some more.

"Here's one for fifty dollars on Amazon," Layla says doubtfully.

"Hold up. I've got one for twenty on eBay. Free shipping." Dan clicks through the product description while Layla and I crowd closer. "It has good reviews. This could be perfect." He glances at me. "I can get it with my mom's account, if you want to just pay me back in cash."

That won't leave me with much left over. But I could afford it. And isn't this why I came—to buy something?

"Yeah, o-okay." I watch Dan check out on eBay, my nerves settling in my gut.

Finished, Dan slips his phone into his pocket. "Maybe I should take it home with me today? The battery will ship to my house. And I still want to do some scans and double-check the hardware, you know."

"Yeah, that works."

Layla grins. "Let's go find the cashier. Then you can buy it!"

"Lead the way." I lift the laptop. Though it's bulkier than those I've seen being used in coffee shops, it's not *that* heavy. We find the cashier. Balancing the laptop in one hand, I fish out my plastic bag of money and pay him on the spot.

"Love your wallet," Dan says, trying to keep a straight face.

"Super fashionable," Layla adds.

"Well, it works." I pass Dan twenty dollars and smile as I pocket the bag again, twenty-five dollars still left. I have something new to trade, and I managed to keep a little bit of my earlier earnings. With my one hand still free, I type a quick note into my trade log. This will work. It's an investment.

We're just about to start searching for Layla's mother when Mrs. Michele comes hurrying into the main hall from the backyard.

"Hi, Mom!" Layla chirps. She and Dan are still smiling.

But my heart freezes. The expression on Mrs. Michele's face is worried, serious. I've seen the look before. The noise of the room dims, my blood beats against my ears, and the laptop presses into my chest as my arms tighten around it.

"Sami," she says. "Your grandfather—you should come."

TRADE LOG

Days: 17

Have: $25

Need: $675

THINGS TO TRADE:

Laptop (waiting on battery)

PLANNED TRADES:

Combat boots for art supplies (Julie)

COMPLETED TRADES:

1. Manchester United key chain -> iPod
2. Coins -> *Game Informer* magazines
3. iPod -> Figurines
4. Figurines -> $145
5. Magazines -> Combat boots

17

"EVERYTHING'S OKAY," MRS. MICHELE KEEPS SAYING to me, a hand on my shoulder as she walks us into the backyard. "He just got dizzy. The fall doesn't seem to have hurt him."

Baba is sitting in the grass with Jared in his lap. Mrs. Michele goes to kneel in front of him, talking, but I can't make out her words anymore. Baba's face is pale, and his hands shake when he pats Jared's head.

Old, goes through my mind. Not the honored, dignified, elderly sort—but old in the Western way. Fragile. Small.

He didn't look like this before we lost the rebab. Before I allowed our past memories and future hopes to be snatched away. I should have held on to them more tightly. Because of my carelessness, Baba is in pain and vulnerable. I put the crack in his spirit, and the gap is spreading from his heart to his health.

I did this.

He sees me. "Ah, Sami jan, it seems I cannot keep up with the kids," he says in Pashto, patting Jared's head again.

I have to wet my lips with my dry tongue before I can speak. In English, I ask, "What happened?"

Baba shrugs. "I had a moment of weakness, but it has passed. I am fine."

"I think he's dehydrated," Mrs. Michele puts in. "But he won't drink. I thought maybe you could help me convince him."

"It's Ramadan." I don't look away from him, not even when I'm answering her. "We're not supposed to eat or drink during the daytime."

"Exactly." Baba's beard brushes Jared's head, and Jared makes a swipe at it.

"But if you're ill—" I try to add.

"I am not ill."

"The ill are exempt."

"I am *not* ill." Baba shakes his head but closes his eyes, as if that alone has made him dizzy again. "I just needed a rest."

But it's not just this, I want to shout at him. *This is*

not dizziness from playing with a child. It is the rebab being gone; it is our music being gone; it is you being at a job you hate, after three years of clawing for safety. I do not know how to heal him. I don't think a doctor would, either. How can you keep someone safe when their heart is breaking? When *you* broke it?

"If you drink, you will feel better," Mrs. Michele says. "Layla, go ask for a glass of water."

Baba frowns like he will argue more, and I don't know what to do but get him to drink. At least water should give him relief from his symptoms, even if it won't solve the problem.

"If you fall again, or something more serious happens, we will have to go to the hospital," I tell him in Pashto. "Drink and be better. God will be understanding."

Baba opens his mouth, but I cut him off. "Please, Baba." What I mean but do not say is: *I can't lose you. You're all I have left.*

The paleness in his face is even more pronounced now. For a moment we just look at each other, and then Baba sighs his agreement. He must be feeling terrible, because he normally would not give in so quickly. Breaking Ramadan—after being unable to participate during our journey—must feel like a failure.

Layla arrives with the water, and I watch Baba drink,

but my chest still hurts from the pounding of my racing pulse. I have to get the rebab, quickly, and nothing I'm doing is enough. The laptop isn't enough.

With a nod to my purchase, Baba says, "You have a laptop now? A laptop and an iPod?"

"Yes," I say, though it's not strictly true. "Dan needs to check it, though."

Baba frowns. "How do you have money for these things?"

"I—uh—"

"I paid for it," Dan cuts in. "But, um, Sami and I will share it for school."

The corners of Baba's mouth lift out of the frown, but stop short of a smile. "Hm. You are becoming a regular American."

"I guess." But that's not true, either.

The water does help Baba, because he starts teasing Jared again, letting the boy crawl on him and try on his white cap. At home, in Afghanistan, he would not have played in public with others people's children. With my cousins, yes—they would sit in his lap while they ate and lean on his shoulder while he tuned the rebab. Family is one thing. But Jared and Layla's family are practically strangers to us.

Those customs changed on the route, when we

traveled beside orphan boys and babies born in ports. We had no family, and so Baba said the world would be our family. I know he is right, yet it hurts me when Jared laughs. The sound is so much like my tiny cousin Navid. Even Baba winces, so slightly that only I see it.

The rebab would dull the pain.

But without it . . .

My legs have become wobbly, and I sit in the grass nearby. *It's not enough*, I keep thinking, over and over and over again. *It's not enough. I'm not doing enough.*

"Your grandfather is so good with Jared, Sami." Suddenly Mrs. Michele is beside me. I was so lost in thought I didn't even hear her approach. "I think Jared might want to stay in your family!"

Baba chuckles. "He would make a good Afghan boy."

I glance between Baba and Jared. How can he call me—his blood and bone—a regular American but say this stranger would make a good Afghan? *I* am his family, not a foreigner.

Jared squeals in delight, and Mrs. Michele grins at me. My anger ebbs into shame. Baba used to watch over many of the children along the route, to give their parents a rest. It doesn't mean anything. The only person acting unusual here is me.

We finally get up and make our way to the car. I

have to support Baba over the uneven lawn. He complains of my over-caution, but his arm trembles as I hold it, and he has to lean on me with every step. Mrs. Michele says he should be fine with water and rest, but my pulse still buzzes in my ears. I tell myself that she is right— he may be better. But deep down I know that he's breaking, more and more every day, and it's up to me to stop it.

While everyone's getting in the van, I tell Mrs. Michele I need to go to the bathroom. But instead, once I'm out of sight, I slip away to a quiet spot on the far side of the street. I fish out the business card, now a little wrinkled, from my pocket.

The last thing I want to do is talk to someone about what happened. I want to keep the memories of before— before the wedding, before the journey—for me and Baba. And I want to forget the most vivid memories—I don't want to think about the event that tore me away.

But Coach said there would be compensation for talking to this man. It's just another trade, really. The sixth trade: my story for funds.

I take my phone and dial.

TRADE LOG

Days: 17

Have: $25

Need: $675

THINGS TO TRADE:

Laptop (waiting on battery)

PLANNED TRADES:

Combat boots for art supplies (Julie)

Story for money (Lincoln Trudeau)

COMPLETED TRADES:

1. Manchester United key chain -> iPod
2. Coins -> *Game Informer* magazines
3. iPod -> Figurines
4. Figurines -> $145
5. Magazines -> Combat boots

18

ON MONDAY AFTER SCHOOL, INSTEAD OF GOING TO THE
rec center, I take the Orange Line to Ruggles. Despite
the knot in my stomach, despite wanting to do anything
but talk about my past—despite everything—I've arranged to meet the PhD student for an interview.

I have to pursue every lead. And right now, while I'm
waiting on the laptop battery and Julie's supplies, this is
the only one I have.

I exit Ruggles Station and blink in the sunlight.
Northeastern University is right in front of me. The traffic noise has died down, and student voices and guitar
music fill the courtyard. Tall buildings covered in shining windows are directly ahead of me. The sky reflects
in the glass, turning the panels vibrant shades of blue and
green. There's a map across the street, and I go to check

that the courtyard on my left is Centennial Common. But before I'm halfway there, I notice a man and a young woman walking toward me.

The man breaks into a grin and calls, "Hello! Are you Sami?"

"Yes, sir." My stomach tightens all over again. "Mr. Trudeau?"

"That's right. But Lincoln is just fine." He holds out his hand, and we shake. His beard is more scruff than anything, almost too blond to be seen against his pale skin. "This is my teaching assistant, Cheryl Mizell."

"Hi!" The young woman, holding a notebook and folders to her chest, makes a little bow. Her purse almost falls off her shoulder when she does, and she barely catches it in time. "Sorry I can't offer a hand."

"Oh, it's okay." I'm actually a little relieved. I'm getting used to playing soccer with girls and riding in the car with women, but shaking hands would feel strange.

"You got all that, Cheryl?" Mr. Lincoln asks, sounding amused.

"Yes, definitely." She smiles apologetically at me. "I'm just about to go to class, but I'll walk with you both to Meserve—it's on the way."

"Meserve Hall is where the interview will happen,"

Mr. Lincoln explains. "Before we go, do you have the permission slip from your grandfather?"

I nod, reaching into my backpack and taking the paper out to hand to him. I slipped it under the forms for the rec center when I had Baba sign them, knowing he was too exhausted to read anything. As I suspected, he just looked for the empty line and left his signature.

It is dishonest—but it's all for the rebab. All to make things right. I try to hide the twinge of guilt while Mr. Lincoln looks over the form.

"Great, this is in order." Mr. Lincoln meets my eyes. "And your grandfather knows where you are, right? He doesn't mind you speaking with me?"

"Right," I say, though it's another lie. Baba believes I am at the rec center. He *probably* wouldn't mind me talking with Mr. Lincoln, but I couldn't really explain why I wanted to without telling him about the trades for the rebab. So I just . . . didn't exactly say where I was going.

"Okay, excellent. On to Meserve, then!" Mr. Lincoln begins to walk. Though Miss Cheryl is dressed in jeans and a blouse, he's wearing a brown suit with a dark blue shirt and red tie. Next to him, I feel sloppy and small in my secondhand school clothes. "It's too hard to find on your own, which is why I thought Centennial would be an easier spot to meet."

I nod, trying to look around without *looking* like I am. The campus is bewildering and huge and full of sounds—shouted laughter, guitar riffs, discussions from students in the oversize outdoor chairs. A mural painted on a brick wall shows a girl with braided hair, paintbrush in one hand and lightning in the other. I want to ask what it means, but I don't want to seem ignorant.

"Have you visited a university before?" Mr. Lincoln asks, waving to some of the students we pass.

"No, sir."

"Well, this is Northeastern." He extends his arms. "It's a bit empty right now. The students here are taking summer classes. The history department is in Meserve Hall, so that's where Cheryl and I spend most of our time. Cheryl's getting a dual degree in history and psychology."

"I'm interested in the way the two relate." Miss Cheryl smiles at me. "I'm thrilled to be working on this project with Professor Trudeau. And it's been wonderful meeting survivors like you."

Survivors. The way she says it makes it sound like a badge of some sort, a title of honor. But it makes me sad.

Before I can figure out why, Mr. Lincoln adds, "We have great science and humanities programs, too. Do you like any subjects in school particularly?"

"I like music," I say, though I'm not sure that's a class subject or something people go to university for.

"Nice!" We turn down a little street, into the shadow of two buildings, and he asks, "What do you play?"

"A rebab."

"The official instrument of Afghanistan!" Miss Cheryl volunteers. "I've been listening to Homayoun Sakhi while I transcribe interviews. Love him!"

I nod, surprised she knows so much. I search for a question to ask in return. "How long have you been studying here, Mr. Lincoln?"

"Two years now." He heads to a large gray door. "The degree might take four or five years, depending on how this dissertation goes. Which—again—*so* excited you're here."

"I need to head this way, Professor Trudeau." Miss Cheryl nods toward the street. "I'll come by after class to see how it went—but I might be late because I have to go to the Geek Squad. Again." She makes a face but frees one hand to give me a quick wave. "Have a good day, Sami."

"You too."

"See you later. Good luck with your virus!" Mr. Lincoln takes me inside to an elevator. "This is super lazy, but the door to the stairs is jammed, so . . ." He shrugs.

We take the elevator to the first floor. Mr. Lincoln

leads me past a red wall with a huge black *1* on it, past an intricate sketch of a crowded street that reminds me of Hamida's work, and to a glass-walled space with a sign that says CAMD CONFERENCE ROOM.

"Come on in." Mr. Lincoln grabs the door for me. "Do you want some water or anything?"

I shake my head.

"Oh, right, Ramadan." He smacks his palm against his forehead. "That was stupid. Let me go put your permission slip in my office and grab something down the hall. Take a seat wherever you want and make yourself at home."

He smiles again and ducks away.

I hesitate as I try to pick somewhere to sit at the long table. In Afghanistan, a guest would be seated in the place of honor, as far from the door as possible, where they would be more comfortable. For an Afghan, especially a Pashtun, the seating arrangement allows the host to protect their guests' lives if someone breaks into the room or house. I know this convention does not matter here, but I still stall, looking at the table, turning the question of where to sit over and over in my head, searching for an answer that does not matter anymore, because I am far from that world. Finally, I slip into a chair midway down the table. I decide to put my back to the glass wall. The windows show the building on the other side of the street, bricks bright in the sunshine.

By the time I've settled, with my backpack near my feet, Mr. Lincoln returns with a plastic bag in one hand, a tissue box in the other, and a notebook, pen, and cell phone balanced on his arm. They don't even wobble while he sets the tissue box down.

"Two years as a waiter come in handy," he says with a wink.

He puts the plastic bag between us. My heart skips. It's full of dried mulberries, Afghan treats I haven't seen since we left.

"I was in DC this weekend." Mr. Lincoln sits in the chair across from me. "They have an Afghan grocery store. Did you know? The Afghan couple I was interviewing recommended these. I figured you would like to wait for iftar to break your fast, so I've made them to go."

It's a kindness I didn't anticipate, and the knot in my stomach loosens. While Mr. Lincoln arranges his things, I study the berries. With this unexpected piece of home, I close my eyes for a moment. I can almost see Kandahar again.

My mor sits on the toshaks after dinner, putting down the plate of snacks. It is divided into different sections, with nakhod in one and cashews in another and wrapped chocolates in the middle. One of the four sections has dried mulberries, my mor's favorite, and after she pours the tea for Plar, Baba, and me, she takes a small handful. We chat about our day while we sit there, around the tablecloth on the floor. The hum of helicopters, on their way to or from war missions, sounds far off beyond the white-painted stone walls. Plar laughs as he tells us funny stories from the base, and Baba offers sage sayings. He claims they are from "the poet," always revered by Pashtuns, but I think he makes some of them up.

My mor jani reaches across the plate to brush dust out of my hair. Were her fingers soft, or callused? Were the bangles on her wrists red and gold, or blue and silver? The color blurs in my head, but the gentle clinks of her bracelets make a song in my ears.

"Okay, so here's the plan."

I blink, and I'm back in Boston. Mr. Lincoln has set his phone, notebook, and pen on the table in front of him. He pauses to align the phone and pencil so that they are evenly spaced from the notebook.

"With your permission, Sami, I'd like to record you on my cell. That will make it easier for me to access the information in the future. I'll also be taking notes. Does that work for you?"

I nod, swallowing to wet my dry throat.

"I'll be asking you some questions, but mostly I'm just here to listen to however much you want to tell. If you ever feel unsafe, or if there's something you are uncomfortable saying, you can say so, and we'll go to a different point or angle. I want you to feel at ease about everything. Yeah?"

I nod again.

"All right, so let's begin." Once he turns on the recording, he sets the phone between us. "Okay, it's June twentieth at"—he checks the clock on the wall behind him—"four o'clock." He faces me. "Can you tell me your name?"

"Sami," I say. I hesitate. I only used my first name when I talked to people on the trek—there was a risk that if our surname leaked it would be a threat to the distant relatives we left behind—and I can't seem to say it now, even though I know that I am safe.

Mr. Lincoln sees my hesitation and says, "First name only is just fine. How old are you?"

"Twelve years old."

He winces but takes a deep breath and writes it down.

"Okay, Sami, what's your story?"

19

"MY PLAR WORKED AS AN INTERPRETER IN KANDAHAR during the war," I begin, feeling it is the right place to start. If he hadn't, would any of the rest have even happened? I might still be in Afghanistan if he had been something else.

"Is that why your English is so good?" Mr. Lincoln asks. "Sorry, I won't interrupt much—your English is just really good."

I nod. "Also, my mor was a flight attendant before I was born. She knew a lot of English, too. They would often speak in English at home—that is how my baba and I became better at it." I pause, glancing at the dried mulberries on the table. I will have to come up with an explanation for them to give Baba—later. But looking at them now helps me remember the better times, the before times. "My mor made up words, just to tease my plar."

And because the sun is out, and because I have mulberries for tonight, and because Mr. Lincoln is the first person eager to listen, and because I do not want to talk about the true beginning of our journey—not yet—I tell him a story from long ago.

The truth is, my mor's English was better than my plar's. She joked with him about it endlessly. Sometimes she would switch to English mid-conversation and use the biggest words she knew. My plar could not always understand and would make her speak more slowly and tell him the meanings.

Once, he came home from the base red-faced and frustrated.

"Zarmina!" He called for my mor. "*Frameire* is *not* an English word!"

She peered from the kitchen innocently. "Oh? It must be French, then."

He shook his head. "I used it with the men today, and they assured me—with many a laugh—that it is not a word *at all*."

"How strange!" she exclaimed carelessly. "I must have dreamed it."

My mor jani was always dreaming.

Though my plar was cross when he came in, he was smiling when he said, "Perhaps you should dream less when you are teaching me."

"Ah, my heart, if I dreamed less, wouldn't you love me less?" My mor lifted her eyebrows and turned to me. "Sami, would you have me dream less?"

I shook my head. "Your dreams are my favorite."

"Even when they are silly?"

"Yes!"

"There, you see? Your son loves my dreams."

My plar rubbed his face. "I would not have you change at all, zama da zra armana. But perhaps you could let me know whether you speak from a dream or from a text-book?"

My mor jani beamed at him, bright and radiant as the summer sun. "I suppose I could."

When she smiled like that, my plar always looked at her in a way I found embarrassing. I returned to my reading to avoid noticing them.

I wish I had paid more attention. Maybe I would remember them better.

Mr. Lincoln laughs through this story, and it makes it easier to begin to talk of the bad times—the fear of the Taliban's return, the years my plar spent trying to get visas so we could leave for America. Some of his friends made it and left ahead of their families to build a new life and smooth the way for them to come. But when an interpreter fled the country, the Taliban often kidnapped sons and brothers and fathers. Sometimes the lost ones were returned for a ransom. If the family could not afford the cost, or could not pay in time, the stolen person was killed.

So my plar wouldn't leave before us. Even when the calls began.

I would find him, sometimes, on the toshaks with his phone in his hand. He would stare into the distance, into our future. I think, now, that he knew what would come. But he would not leave us. He kept trying.

Even with his English, even with Sergeant Pycior's help, my plar could not get his applications approved. The forms just became longer and longer. The politics became more and more complicated.

"Then, in the spring, one of my cousins got married." I pause. My palms sweat. My skin crawls. The table seems to grow and press against my chest, and I imagine people are peering through the glass walls at my back. I glance over my shoulder. No one is there. Where is the exit? How will I escape if the door to the stairs is jammed? Would the bathroom across the hall be safe, or would they search there first?

This room has no protection. Someone could shoot straight through that glass. It's probably not blast proof. Anything would shatter it.

"Hey, Sami?" Mr. Lincoln says gently. "How are you feeling?"

I turn around again and try to swallow the lump in my throat. "I'm fine," I answer automatically. But my hands are shaking on the table. I'm cold and hot at once.

"You don't have to talk about the wedding," he says. "You're in charge of the conversation. Maybe we should skip ahead?"

But I should be able to say it. After all, three years have passed. And there is no one looking for me here.

Still, my body and my heart don't understand how to remember right. They only know how to relive the bad stuff over and over and over again, until it feels like it's happening in this room, right now. I wish my body could remember how it felt when my plar was happy. I wish my ears could relive my mor's laugh in the same stark, vivid way. Instead, my memories of *before* keep fading, only coming clear at random, while the memory of the wedding always lurks, like a wave in the back of my mind waiting to pull me under.

I feel like I *should* be able to say it, but Mr. Lincoln says I don't have to, so I force the bad memories to return to hiding. It takes me a few seconds to find where the story turns safe again. "We—just Baba and I—took a bus to Nimruz. It's southwest of Kandahar, where you can find smugglers to take you across the border."

They charged us nearly all our savings. The last truck had been shot at, and a few passengers had died before the rest were deported back to Afghanistan. Others who tried the crossing were beheaded, or tangled in the barbed wire, or simply lost. Using a smuggler did not mean we would be safe, but going through the treacherous, brutally guarded terrain without one was almost certain death.

We went, and God blessed our path. We reached Iran and stayed a month in our relatives' back room. Once we had rested, we started hearing the whispers of Europe. Hope.

As I tell my story, the words take me over. It's like I'm the instrument, and they are playing me, saying things I did not know, things I had forgotten. They rush on, even when I want to close my mouth, even when I want to cry. They have to get out. I can't control them. Mr. Lincoln isn't even asking questions—it's just me, talking and talking and talking, trying to get to the end.

We made it to Turkey and then took the boat to Greece. Everything was chaos, and we lived in a public park for a few days before we found an affordable, cramped hostel room. We shared it with twenty other men while we waited for money to be wired from a distant uncle in Kabul.

Then we happened to meet Sergeant Pycior again, now discharged and working with a nonprofit. He convinced us America might still work. It wasn't too late to fulfill Plar's dream for us to live there.

"They're saying the borders out of Greece will close soon," he told us, "and the atmosphere is already strained. America would be better."

He helped us return safely to Istanbul, where it was marginally more comfortable to live, even though Baba wasn't allowed to work. Over the next three years he helped us with the visa applications. He had contacts in the States, and he did everything he could in honor of my plar.

Finally, we came to America. We had a few weeks to get settled, with the help of our placement agency, but then the rebab was stolen. I finish my story by explaining my quest. The words fade, leaving the room silent. My whole body aches. My lungs heave like I've been running or sobbing. My bones feel loose and jiggly. Mr. Lincoln's eyes are red. I don't know when he cried. I am more tired than I've ever felt in my entire life.

Mr. Lincoln opens and closes his mouth. Finally, he says softly, "I don't have any words."

I lower my gaze, unsure if I should apologize, unsure how to respond. A heaviness hangs in the air, expectant.

Mr. Lincoln turns off the recording. He pauses, exhales. "You've broken my heart, Sami." Then he bends until I have to meet his eyes. "Thank you. Thank you for sharing your story with me."

Maybe I should thank him for listening, or asking, or being so kind. But I am too tired. I do not have anything left to say. I've exhausted all of my English. I just nod.

"It might have a better ending by Eid al-Fitr," I finally say to fill the silence. "Inshallah."

"Inshallah," Mr. Lincoln echoes, smiling faintly. Then he digs in his pocket. "*I'm* tired now, so you must be completely done in. I have compensation for you, but I'm afraid it's not that much. I wish I had more to give."

He passes fifty dollars to me. That's half the price of the computer earned back. *Not too bad*, I think, though I'm so exhausted I hardly know what to feel. I thank him softly as I add it to my plastic bag of funds. His smile gets a little wider.

"Hold on!" he exclaims, springing to his feet. "I have an idea. Wait a second."

He's out the door before I know how to respond. I turn in my chair to watch him run down the hallway. All my muscles hurt. I'll have enough trouble just getting through my homework before iftar and bed.

Mr. Lincoln returns after a few minutes, four heavy-looking books in his hands. He sets them down with a thud on the table.

"These are textbooks I've kept since my master's degree," he says. He taps the spines. "I'm a bit of a sentimental sap, but I don't need them. If you want, you can take them to sell—that should get you about a hundred or more, I imagine. Would that help?"

I blink in surprise. "I don't—I shouldn't—If fifty dollars is what you're giving everyone—"

"Seriously, you would be doing me a favor." Mr. Lincoln smiles. "These things keep getting in the way in my office—that is, my advisor's office. We have to share a space, and we're both pack rats. If it's up to me, I'll be holding these books until the day I die. If you take them, you'll be saving me a lot of trouble!"

A smile tugs on my mouth. "Okay, I guess."

"Here, let's see if we can squeeze them into your backpack."

We manage it, though by the end my bag weighs almost as much as I do. Mr. Lincoln adds the mulberries to an outside pocket and then helps me lift it on. All the way downstairs and to the courtyard, he teases me about being careful to not break my back.

Once we're outside, Mr. Lincoln points to Ruggles Station. He asks, "Think you can get home from here?"

"Yes, thanks." I shift the straps, trying to ease the weight off my shoulders. "Da khuday pa aman—I leave you in God's peace."

Mr. Lincoln hooks his thumbs on his suit pockets. "Da khuday pa aman," he says in a clumsy attempt at the phrase.

I hesitate, smiling. "Actually, it is the person leaving who always says, *Da khuday pa aman*—the person staying replies, *Pu mukha de sha*."

"Oh!" He beams. "What does that mean?"

"May you face only good."

Mr. Lincoln becomes more serious. "Pu mukha de sha, then. I do hope you have many good things ahead, Sami."

I bow my head out of habit, then turn toward the station. Though I'm carrying my weight in books, I feel just a little bit lighter.

Six trades. I'm drawing closer to the rebab.

TRADE LOG

Days: 15

Have: $75

Need: $625

THINGS TO TRADE:

Laptop (waiting on battery)

PLANNED TRADES:

Combat boots for art supplies (Julie)

Textbooks for money

COMPLETED TRADES:

1. Manchester United key chain -> iPod
2. Coins -> *Game Informer* magazines
3. iPod -> Figurines
4. Figurines -> $145
5. Magazines -> Combat boots
6. Story -> $50 + textbooks

20

TWO DAYS LATER, THE BELL RINGS ON THE LAST CLASS
of the school year. I weave around yelling kids, grab the
stuff from my locker, and hurry to meet Dan by the basketball court.

"We made it!" he shouts, holding up his hand.

I high-five him without hesitating. I can hardly believe I've survived to the end of the term. Tests are done,
and I think I did all right. For a few months, I won't have
any more classes. I won't have to worry about Peter glar-
ing at my back. Instead, I can focus all my attention on
getting the rebab.

Dan waves to some of his other friends as we make
our way past the court and the playground. "Okay, where
are we at with the trades?"

"Julie's bringing her art supplies to practice today

and I'll trade her for the combat boots. Then I want to show the art supplies to Hamida."

"Wicked." Dan bounces his backpack higher on his shoulders as we round onto the sidewalk and pause at the crosswalk. A bunch of other students are gathered there to wait.

"The laptop battery shipped, finally," Dan adds. The light changes from a red hand to a walking person. Most of the others turn left to the corner store, but we cross toward the mechanic's shop. Dan has to raise his voice above the machinery. "It's supposed to be here Friday afternoon. I've finished all the virus scans and stuff on the laptop, so it'll be good to go as soon as the battery arrives."

"Okay. And then we list it on eBay?" I try not to sound too anxious. The battery is taking longer to come than I thought it would, and I don't have much time to make up the money I spent on the laptop.

"Yep."

We come to the other side of the shop, out of sight of the school. A group of kids is farther on, but it's less crowded overall. Loud steps follow us, composing a beat in my head.

The beat quickens. I turn.

Peter's right behind me, but he doesn't look my way. "Hey, Dan."

Dan stares straight ahead, not acting surprised. "Hey, Pete."

"Good riddance to seventh grade, am I right?" Peter walks on the other side of Dan. He waves back toward the building. "See ya, detention-prison!"

Dan ignores him and says to me instead, "Do you know when the next trade will be?"

I glance between them, the unspoken tension making my muscles bunch up under my skin. I don't want them to fight like they did about the iPod. "Um, it depends on if Hamida is interested in the art supplies. We can figure it out today, though."

"Cool. Let me know."

"Dan, did you see Justin puke after laps on Tuesday?" Peter cuts in. "It was awesome."

"Yeah. It was funny, I guess." Dan shrugs and turns into the rec center courtyard.

Peter keeps pace, and an uneasy realization dawns on me. He's coming with us. I joined at the start of the month, when Peter couldn't play. Of course he's back now. He's the regular—I'm the temporary, the fill-in.

The glass building flashes in the sun, the tarmac warm—familiar—beneath my shoes. I clench my backpack straps in my hands and stand straighter. I'm on this team now, and I don't have to be afraid.

Besides. There's no reason Peter and I can't be on the same side.

The bell chimes as Dan opens the door. Miss Juniper is at the desk talking with Coach. She laughs at something he says and then smiles at us. "Good afternoon. Oh, hello, Peter."

"Hi." Peter snatches the clipboard as soon as Dan's done and signs in before me.

"I'll see you guys back there in a minute," Coach says. "So, Juniper, did you finish the book on Iceland? What did you think about . . ."

After I write my information, I walk toward the hallway. Dan follows me, frowning at Coach and Miss Juniper.

"Weird," Dan mutters.

"Do Coach and Juniper have a thing?" Peter asks.

Dan shrugs.

"*Weird*," Peter agrees.

I open the door to the gym and go inside. Most of the team is already clustered in smaller groups talking. Their voices echo in the large room, and I catch bits of conversation about summer break and the Fourth of July. Dan dumps his backpack by the wall, and Peter puts his down beside it. I set mine next to Julie's, so I can be sure to trade with her—my seventh trade—before we leave. It's easy to spot her bag because it's covered in army patches.

Peter keeps on Dan's heels. "So, Dan, my mom is going to rent *Super Smash Bros.* next week. You want to come over and play it?"

"Can't. Sami and I have plans."

"For the whole *week*?" Peter glares at me. "What're you doing this time? Burning some American flags?"

I flinch.

Dan clenches his fists. "If you just tried to *not* be a racist moron and asked Sami *nicely*, maybe I'd tell you."

Peter's eyes harden. He's ready for a fight.

This conflict has to be defused before it gets worse. I don't really trust Peter with the truth about the rebab and the trades, but I have to find some way to calm him down. "I'm trying to get back something that was stolen," I blurt out. "You are welcome to help if you'd like."

Both Peter and Dan look at me, startled.

"There would still be time for *Super Smash Bros.*, probably," I suggest.

Peter scowls. "No offense, but I didn't invite you."

"No offense," Dan snaps, "but that's pretty offensive."

"Dan, it's fine," I try to cut in. I need them to stop arguing. If they get me into trouble again, Baba may ask more about my time at the rec center, and someone might let it slip about the trades.

"It's *not* fine." Dan glares at Peter. "If you can't be a decent human being, stay out of it."

"*I'm* your friend, Dan!" Peter jabs a finger at me. "*He's* changed you."

"Yeah, well, so what?"

"What is your *problem*?" Peter snaps. "Is this still about the vandalism thing? I did my time! It's over! And anyway, if I remember right, you were going to do it, too."

I look at Dan, surprised.

His face turns a guilty red. "But I *didn't*."

"Yeah, because you conveniently 'got sick.'" Peter makes air quotes. "You backed out as soon as it got real because you didn't have the guts to stick around."

"It was a stupid idea! If you wanted to get back at Jim for framing you with the bracelet, you should've done something half-brained about *him*, not Ms. Nolan."

"Well, if you had actually *been there*, maybe you could've said that!"

Other team members are noticing now, and some start to drift our way. Layla jogs over, glancing from me to the others uncertainly. But I don't understand what's going on any better than she does. This fight isn't about me anymore.

"Then you start hanging around with this guy!" Peter points at me. If he notices the rest of the team, the audience only encourages him. "What would your dad think if he knew you were buds with this Arab?"

Dan's voice tightens into a hiss. "I don't know. If you can find him, you can ask."

"Won't be hard. I'll just look anywhere you're *not*. Like his girlfriend's house." Peter shakes his head, but there's a smirk in the corner of his mouth. "You break your promises, then take off whenever you want. You're turning into him."

Dan shouts a cuss word and jumps forward. Peter dodges. Dan's fist narrowly misses his jaw. I shove between them. Dan's second punch lands on my shoulder. I push a hand against his chest to hold him back. Layla grabs Dan's arm.

"Cool it!" Benj says from the sidelines.

"Sock him! Sock him!" some of the others chant.

"Stop!" I shout in Dan's face. "You'll just get yourself in trouble."

"Uh-huh, the terrorist will keep you safe!" Peter says from behind me. "Until he blows you up!"

Dan tries to wrench out of Layla's hold, and my wrist cracks with keeping him in place. "Say that again!"

"Shut up, both of you," Layla snaps.

"Benj, get Coach!" I call, catching his eye. He nods and runs for the door.

"Let me go!" Dan tries to pull away again. "He's asking for it!"

"You're my friend!" I yell. "I'm not letting you get into trouble."

For the barest second, the length it takes me to suck another breath, the word settles in my bones. *Friend*, what Dan said so easily the first time we came to the rec center, when we were still strangers. The word I'm thinking in Pashto—*wror*—is closer to blood brother than classmate. Weeks ago, such a friendship would have frightened me—before, it has always come with loss. But now it warms me and makes me feel strong. "I'm not letting you get hurt!"

"Get out of the way, Sami!" Dan snaps.

Coach comes running in, Benj on his heels. "What's going on?"

Both Peter and Dan step back, suddenly silent and sullen.

"Peter's being a real jerk!" Layla jumps in. "He called Sami a terrorist."

Others volunteer bits of the fight as testimony. I stay between Dan and Peter, just in case one of them still tries something. The longer Coach listens, the more he frowns. When they finish, he turns to Peter.

"This is a violation of our honor code, Peter. It's

unacceptable," he says, flat and direct. "I'm going to ask you to leave. Speak with Juniper on your way out, and she can give you a letter for your mother. We will have to figure out the terms for you to be allowed to come back. Layla, you go with him."

"But—!" Peter protests.

Coach shakes his head. "I'm not discussing it. Go."

Peter looks from me to the others. They stare back at him coldly. I have a feeling that it will be easier for him to overcome the rec center's requirements to get reinstated than to earn the team's forgiveness. Peter seems to sense this, too. He clenches his jaw and stomps out. Layla follows.

"Dan, you know we don't allow fights here," Coach says, turning to him. "But considering it didn't get physical, I think we'll let it slide. Just this once."

Dan lowers his gaze. "Yes, sir."

Coach nods and motions to the others. "Okay, everyone, let's warm up!"

I normally jog in the front when we do laps, but now I hang near the middle with Dan. I can't stop thinking of the things Peter said during the fight. I hadn't noticed them before, because he hides them really well, but Dan has war scars, too. Scars his dad brought back, whether he wanted to or not. Maybe they're not as deep or as clear as mine, but they're there. Even now, as we run side by side around the track, I see them in the way he tilts his head away from me.

For the first loop around the court, we don't talk.

"Hey, Sami?" Dan says between pants as we start the second loop.

"Yeah?"

"Thanks."

Coach pulls Dan aside after practice. I hesitate, waiting to see if Dan needs me, but Coach's voice is soft and kind. Dan isn't in trouble, so I go to join Julie. She pulls her bin of art supplies out of her large backpack. "Here, have a look and see what you think."

Inside the bin are markers and brushes and paints. They look fancier than the supplies at school and seem hardly used, but I don't actually have any idea what they're worth. I look up to find Hamida and see that she's wandered near us curiously, as if the art supplies are calling to her.

"Hamida," I call, and wave her to join us, "want to check this out?"

Grinning, Hamida drops down beside the bin. "This

is awesome!" she exclaims, pushing around the stuff to get a better look at everything. "Julie, these are so cool!"

"Thanks." Julie shrugs. "I threw in some of the art books from camp, too."

"Really?" Hamida starts digging.

"So, you want to trade?" I ask Hamida, hopeful.

"Yes! Definitely." She leans back on her heels to grin at Julie and me. "You know—my brother just got a new guitar and said I can have his old one if I want it. But I'd way rather practice drawing. So how about that for this?"

"Great." I pull the combat boots from my bag and hold them out to Julie. "Trade?"

"Trade," she says, taking them.

Hamida puts the lid back on the art supplies and passes them to me. "I'll bring the guitar on Friday—we can exchange them after prayer, okay?"

"Perfect."

I pick up the bin. It's too big for my backpack, but that's all right—I can carry it in my arms. I'll tell Baba someone at school loaned me the supplies for a summer project, which is true enough. Layla comes over to chat with Hamida and Julie. I wave to them as I head out.

Dan catches me by the door. "What'd I miss?"

"Hamida's going to trade a guitar." Dan and I walk

through the lobby. Thinking out loud, I say, "I bet I could sell that at Creature Guitars."

"Nice!" Dan pulls out his phone. "Let me check how much it might go for."

"Good idea." I grin.

"Mmm, looks like—depending on the brand—it should be about ninety dollars. Just don't let the owner guy talk you lower than seventy-five."

"Okay. Maybe I can check on the rebab while I'm there," I add, getting excited. "Hey—if you want to come, I could show it to you."

"Yes!" Dan's face brightens, and he looks more like himself—the last of the shadow from the fight vanishing. "Definitely."

I nod, pleased. After all Dan has done, he deserves to see what the trades are for.

Besides. He's my friend.

TRADE LOG

Days: 13

Have: $75

Need: $625

THINGS TO TRADE:

Laptop (waiting on battery)

PLANNED TRADES:

Art supplies for guitar (Hamida)

Textbooks for money

COMPLETED TRADES:

1. Manchester United key chain -> iPod
2. Coins -> *Game Informer* magazines
3. iPod -> Figurines
4. Figurines -> $145
5. Magazines -> Combat boots
6. Story -> $50 + textbooks
7. Combat boots -> Art supplies

21

IN THE MOSQUE'S INDOOR COURTYARD, I STAND AGAINST
the parking lot doors, waiting for the Friday prayer to
begin. Baba, near me, occasionally murmurs greetings to
those who pass us. He always feels it's important to visit
with the members, to start learning more about this place
we've landed in. But today, like most days now, he is not
talkative.

Digging in my pocket, I pull out my phone and check
my note app. I like reading through my list even though
I have it memorized. Eleven days left. I don't have to check
my calendar to know—it's stuck in my head like my
brain's a countdown clock. Eleven days to raise $625.

A text pops up on my screen. It's from Hamida: *Got
the guitar in my dad's trunk. Meeting you and Dan at the
rec center, right?*

I glance around. She's standing only a few people away. I type: *Yes. Dan's got to take the guitar home with him. And you know you can just talk to me?*

But then your grandfather might suspect something! This is a TOP SECRET surprise Eid mission.

Around me, people are heading toward the big room for prayers. I stick my phone in my pocket, and only then do I realize that Baba has been watching me. His expression is sad. But he's always sad now, a little more every day since I lost the rebab.

I pick up the bin of art supplies from near my feet, and we enter along the left-hand side, past where the women sit. When we pause to slip off our shoes and put them in the cubbies, I stuff the bin beside our sandals. I follow Baba into the center of the main room. The mosque is big, with gleaming white walls, flooded with sunlight, clean and empty. I visited the Hagia Sophia while we lived in Turkey, and though it was much grander than this and covered with gold mosaic, it felt darker, somehow. This mosque is more comfortable and friendly. The green carpet is bristly under my socks, tugging them a little with every step.

There's a space in the back for two.

The imam begins his lesson. This week, it's on the subject of prayer. This imam is new to this mosque and considered very modern, and I like the way he uses stories to make his points more real. But sitting still makes my fingers fidget, and my mind won't concentrate.

My thoughts wander back to the stolen rebab. My fault.

Eleven days and $625 left. My only chance to make it right.

My gaze drifts as I think, and I notice Baba's hands resting on his knees beside me. They have always been wrinkled across the smooth backs, while his fingertips are callused from years of playing a stringed instrument. But dark cracks streak painfully over his skin now, like dry desert ground. Some of them look as if they've been bleeding.

It's from the dishes job. He has joked about the soap being cheaper than the stuff the aid agencies gave us in Greece, which hurt him enough. I imagine those cracks on my hands, imagine what it must feel like to get soap and water in them constantly, the way they'd sting and burn.

This is why I have to make the trades work.

The rebab will get him out of this job. But more—it will mend the crack in his spirit.

The imam concludes his talk, and we stand for the namaz. The congregation, led by our imam, recites the prayer in Arabic, beginning with "God is great," *Allahu Akbar*.

We stay standing for the first two parts, then bow toward the qibla before we kneel. My voice blends with everyone else's, the soft rhythm like a lullaby. I press my forehead to the carpet two times and then sit up straight. The familiar movements calm my racing mind, and as we pass the minutes in the routine, a sliver of ease slips past my guilt at losing the rebab and my worries about the $625, and soothes my anxious chest.

To end the prayer, we turn to our right and left to say, "May the peace and mercy of God be upon you." It's meant to be a blessing to angels and the others in the room. I wish it for Baba.

After we're dismissed, I help Baba stand and steady him while he shifts his stiff legs. As we wait in line to get our shoes again, people chatter happily around us. Baba and I don't talk—I imagine our silence looks like a hole in the loud room.

I busy myself putting on my shoes so we can return to the main lobby.

"I need to wash my hands, Sami," Baba says, patting my shoulder. "Wait by the shop so I can find you again."

"All right." This time, I don't remind him it's called "going to the bathroom" here. While he heads in the other direction, I tuck the bin of art supplies under one arm and skirt around the edge of the crowd to the shop near the entrance. I stand with my back to the decorative plates and glance at the electric sign above the door. WELCOME! scrolls across it in brightly colored lights.

Some of the members greet me as they pass. One woman in a hijab laughs when she sees me peering in the store's direction. "Don't buy anything in there—it is far overpriced!"

I smile and thank her, but I can't stop looking at the shop. There's a poster for Adam Travel beside the door, with a picture of pilgrims on the hajj. Inside, the shop is crowded with veils and vases and shirts.

It makes me think of Kandahar Air Field, the base where my plar did most of his translating. He brought me there to see the boardwalk once. It was a wooden walk-way that made a square at the center of the base, with a field hockey pitch in the middle. The boardwalk was lined with American restaurants like TGI Fridays, Pizza Hut, and KFC, but the TGI Fridays was actually owned by an Afghan. Sergeant Pycior always worried about the Tim Horton's, which rumor said would leave when the Canadians did. I still remember biting into one of those donuts, after what felt like hours waiting in line—the sugary softness of the bread and the frosting flaking off on my fingers.

The boardwalk also had small stalls for Afghan jewelry, purses made from chadari fabric, iPad covers woven by nomads, and other wares. My father used to chuckle over the prices—three or five times more expensive than in the regular markets.

"Assalamu alaikum, Sami!"

I blink away the memory. Mr. Farid is standing in front of me. Behind him, Hamida waves excitedly, points at the bin under my arm, and dashes out. I hope Baba doesn't take too long—I need to be at the rec center in a few minutes for the trade. "Walaikum assalam. How are you, Mr. Farid?"

"Doing well. How are you and your grandfather?"

I hesitate, thinking of Baba's hands. "We are . . . all right."

Mr. Farid tilts his head. "I've missed his music in the station. Do you think he will play there again?"

A lump rises in my throat, and I try to swallow it down. I lower my eyes, but Mr. Farid has already noticed how I'm struggling to reply. I glance at the door and see Baba walking toward us. "Ask Hamida. She can explain."

Mr. Farid looks confused, but before he can ask

more questions, I greet Baba and say, "Mr. Farid and I were just talking about the service."

I look up at Mr. Farid, hoping he won't mind the slight exaggeration.

For a moment he hesitates. Then offers, "Your grandson had some rather astute observations." He gives me a subtle nod before turning his smile to Baba. "I hope you are doing well."

"Yes, thank you." Baba's voice can't hide the tired note, like a minor key trying to play itself major.

Someone calls to Mr. Farid, and he waves. "I'm afraid I must go, but I hope to see you next Friday. May your Ramadan be blessed—only eleven days till Eid al-Fitr!"

"Pa mukha de gulunah," Baba says for good-bye.

"Have a good week, Mr. Farid," I add.

Baba turns to me as Mr. Farid walks away. "He is a kind man." His eyes brighten, and he lifts his eyebrows. "What did you notice in the service?"

My phone dings, saving me from making up some "astute observations."

"Oh, sorry." I pull it out. "Just a moment."

I turn away from Baba to read the text from Dan that flashes on the screen: *At the rec center. Hamida here. WHERE ARE YOU???*

Coming, I type. Then I glance at Baba. "I need to leave for practice."

"You are always hurrying off, Sami jan."

The gentle admonishment in his words stings, and I shift from one foot to the other. "I'm really sorry. I'll make the meal for iftar tonight."

My phone dings with a new message: *GOTTA PLAY A GAME BUT COME!!!* Then it dings with about twenty random emojis sent one after the other.

"Please, can I go?" I ask Baba while I type an excuse to Dan.

Baba sighs. "Very well. I have to return to the restaurant anyway."

"Okay, see you later." I hurry to the door.

I don't even think about looking back.

"Sami!" When I come into the rec center gym, Dan breaks away from the game, practically hopping with excitement. "Coach—Coach, can we do a time-out, real quick?"

Coach smiles and blows his whistle. "All right, everyone. Two-minute time-out."

Dan runs over, followed by Layla and Hamida. Hamida grabs the guitar case by her backpack and shoves it at me.

"Here, here!" she says, snatching the bin from my hands and leaving me with the guitar in my arms. "Trade done! Look at all this loot, Layla!"

I blink and smile, while Layla and Hamida bend over the bin. "That was easy."

"Yeah, totally—but look!" Dan holds his phone out so close to my face I can't see anything but a blur. "The laptop battery came this morning!"

I push his arm back so I can actually see. The screen shows a page on eBay, and my laptop is in the picture next to a listing for $220. The Buy It Now option is set to five hundred dollars.

Surprised, I say, "Wow, you already listed it?"

"Yep. Those prices okay? I think it will go for higher than two hundred twenty dollars—people have to bid up from there. I put it up for a five-day run to start, see how that goes."

My heart hammers with something between nervousness and excitement. I invested so much into that laptop—it has to be worth it.

I put the guitar next to Dan's backpack. "You still okay to take this home for me? No way Baba wouldn't notice. Then maybe we could go to Creature Guitar tomorrow?"

"Can't go tomorrow. Got a court thing." Dan says without looking up from his phone. Shrugging, he puts it down by his stuff. "But Monday would work."

"Thirty seconds!" Coach calls. "I need everyone back on the field."

"Come o—" Layla calls, but the last word is lost in a nasty-sounding cough. She runs to her spot anyway.

"Thanks, Sami!" Hamida says, punching my shoulder as she runs to take her place by Layla.

Eight trades done, and I have *three* leads now—the guitar, textbooks, and laptop. Plus I'll see the rebab myself in a few short days. For the first time in weeks, I feel like the trades will work—like I'll actually bring the rebab home—and Baba won't be sad anymore. Everything will be better.

"Ten seconds!"

"You're on my team." Dan shoves me ahead of him. "Offense. Go!"

I stumble into the game, laughing.

TRADE LOG

Days: 11

Have: $75

Need: $625

THINGS TO TRADE:

Laptop (now listed on eBay!)

PLANNED TRADES:

Textbooks for money

Guitar for money

COMPLETED TRADES:

1. Manchester United key chain -> iPod
2. Coins -> *Game Informer* magazines
3. iPod -> Figurines
4. Figurines -> $145
5. Magazines -> Combat boots
6. Story -> $50 + textbooks
7. Combat boots -> Art supplies
8. Art supplies -> Guitar

22

ON MONDAY, I WAKE UP TO A TEXT FROM DAN: *Hey! Mom FREAKED after the court thing! She's dragging me off to New York to see Gran. Sorry!!*

My stomach turns with unease at the delay, but I text him back immediately. *Thanks for letting me know. Is everything okay?*

His reply doesn't come for a few hours. *Yeah. LOOK I FOUND A DEAD LIZARD IN MY GRAN'S GARAGE!*

I still don't understand what happened at court, but I drop it. The next few days, I hang out at the rec center—playing soccer, working on my English reading with a tutor, watching our eBay ad in the computer lab. So far the ad hasn't received *any* bids. It isn't even being watched. Dan sends me a steady stream of texts with different pictures of weird things he's finding in his grandmother's house: plastic rabbit statues, moldy comic books, an eight-box collection of *Better Homes & Gardens* magazines . . .

He doesn't mention the court events. I try to write a text to ask, but it sounds awkward and pushy. I hope he knows I'd listen. But if he wants to be distracted, I can help with that, too.

Finally, on Wednesday night he comes back into town, and *finally*, on Thursday, Dan and I meet at Roxbury Crossing Station instead of going to practice. I'm buzzing with anticipation. I have the textbooks in my backpack, and he has the guitar over his shoulder. I'll sell them all today. But even better: I'll finally get to see the rebab again. I can hardly keep from bouncing my feet on the T, I'm so wound up with excitement. When Dan and I get off at Porter Station, I nearly jump with every step. We head down the street toward the shop, Dan talking about a recent soccer tournament.

"You sure you're okay missing practice?" I ask. Even in my excitement, I can't help being surprised he was so willing to go with me instead of play a game.

"Yeah, I hear Layla's still out, anyway," he says with a shrug. "It'd be way too easy to beat the others without her."

I'm not sure it would be *that* easy, but there has definitely been a lack of challenge since Layla came down with a cold on Monday.

My phone dings, and Dan's plays a clip of rock music at the same time. We both look. Mine has a text from Layla. It's a picture of a hand-drawn card. I make the image bigger and read:

My parents & I cordially invite you
to celebrate the
FOURTH OF JULY
with us next week
on the FOURTH OF JULY.
There will be fireworks and food and music.
The quintessential American experience!

A second ding and a second text appears: *I wanted to make fancy invitations but I didn't have time to mail them, so here you go. Also I didn't want you to catch my cold, which is *definitely* going to be over by the 4th. COME SHED PATRIOTIC TEARS WITH US.*

"Wicked," Dan says, glancing up from his screen. "You got the invite from Layla?"

I nod. "Patriotic tears?"

"Yeah, she's being weird." Dan types an answer, then

sticks his phone in his pocket. "Are you gonna go? You should. It's awesome. Last year, one of the fireworks was smiley-face shaped."

"I don't know. July Fourth is right before my deadline." Besides, as long as the crescent moon is sighted, Ramadan will end at sunset on the fifth. It feels a bit wrong to be gone for one of the last fast-breakings—when Baba and I are both so close to finishing our fasting, each iftar should be special. Maybe I could convince Baba to go with us . . . "I don't have much time before I need to have the rebab for Eid al-Fitr."

Before Dan can answer, a third text arrives: *GUYS GUYS ALSO my dad and I were talking and I THINK HE WANTS TO GET MY MOM A LAPTOP FOR HER BIRTHDAY! I told him we have one and he'd like to look it over!*

My pulse quickens. So far, nothing has happened on the eBay listing. This could be the solution.

"Awesome!" Dan grins. "See, now you *have* to come. It's the perfect chance to sell the laptop! Then you'll have completed all the trades before Eid al—al-Fitter."

"Eid al-Fitr."

"Right. That. What's that, again?"

I have to smile. "The celebration after Ramadan ends. It's not too different from your Christmas—we give gifts

209

and spend time with family and have big celebrations that last days. Or, we did at home, anyway."

"Got it. And what day is that again?"

"Should be the sixth."

"Okay, then you *have* to come to the Fourth of July! It's not *too* close. Besides, it's going to be a blast."

I wince a little at his choice of words. But he has a point—the event would be a convenient way to trade the laptop. I can't afford to pass up any opportunity—especially since the eBay sale isn't looking promising. After all, I took a chance with Mr. Lincoln, and that went well.

And I'm curious. I've heard about the celebrations for the Fourth of July and seen them in movies. It would be fun to go.

"I'll think about it," I promise. Then I add, "But I'll probably go."

"Yessss." Dan gives me a thumbs-up.

We arrive at the used-book store. Inside, a college student sits behind the counter, studying an open notebook and stack of index cards, but he shoots us a smile. When I set my heavy backpack on his desk, he chuckles. "Here to sell, I take it?"

"Yes, please." I unzip the top and lift out the bulky books one by one. The student logs in to his computer and scans codes off the back covers.

"Okay, let's see. *Methodological Approaches to Community-Based Research*," the student mutters, typing. Then he pauses to flip through the pages. "Minor markings. We could give you forty dollars for this."

I nod. Forty dollars for a book seems like a lot to me.

"*Pakistan on the Brink*. No markings. How about sixty dollars?"

My eyes widen. I nod again.

"*Migration Across Boundaries*. Minor markings. Let's go with . . . seventy-five dollars?"

Dan elbows me excitedly. I can hardly believe this.

"And, last one—*The Warmth of Other Suns*." The student opens the front flap of the book and grins excitedly. "Signed! How cool is that?"

"Signed?" I echo, leaning over to look. In loopy writing are the words: *To Lincoln, Warmest wishes and God bless your own research! Good luck—and feel free to reach out!* I didn't realize he'd given me something like this—something so personal.

"There's only light bumps to the spine. Looks like whoever had this took good care of it." The student types some more. "I could give you thirty dollars. Sound good?"

I just stare, trying to add up the numbers in my head, trying to take in that Mr. Lincoln gave me *so much* and pretended like *I* was doing *him* a favor.

"That's great!" Dan volunteers for me.

The student does some more typing and then pulls cash out of the register. "Okay. Then that's two hundred and five dollars altogether. Here you go."

My fingers close around the wad of cash. I barely manage to croak, "Thank you."

"Yeah, have a good day!" Dan grabs my empty backpack, turns me toward the door, and pushes me forward, almost like he thinks the student might change his mind. Once we're in the street, he gasps, "Holy cow."

I carefully fold the wad and put it in my little plastic-bag wallet. Two hundred and five plus my seventy-five equals two hundred and eighty dollars. The numb surprise is wearing off, and my pulse starts buzzing with excitement. Trade nine: *way* more successful than I could have imagined.

My head feels light with the rush of good luck—and Mr. Lincoln's generosity—and I let out a relieved laugh. "Okay. That was—Wow."

"Come on, we've got to hit up the next place while we're on a streak!" Dan starts off down the street. The music shop is only about three blocks down. The GUI-TARS WANTED sign still sits in the window. Dan shifts the guitar case while I grab the door and hold it open. The bell chirps as we march in.

The owner sits behind the counter with another car magazine. "Welcome to Creature Guitar," he says while he finishes reading his sentence. Finally, he glances up. "Come to sell something?"

Dan and I make our way to him. I answer, "Yes, I have a guitar to sell. But I also—We spoke a few weeks ago about my rebab?"

"Oh, right. I remember. You got the money?"

"No, but I will soon—by the fifth."

Dan slides the guitar off his shoulder and lifts it onto the counter. "Not like you deserve it," he mutters, so quiet even I barely hear.

I nudge him in warning, raising my voice to say, "I was hoping I could see the rebab, though?"

"Sure, kid. Let's look at this first."

The man lifts the guitar out of the case. We wait while he turns the instrument over, examining it from a few angles and occasionally making a small grunt. Rock music plays on the speakers, turned down low enough that only the high notes sound clear. I shift from foot to foot, trying to hide my nerves.

Finally, the man returns the guitar to its case. "Okay. I can give you seventy dollars."

"One hundred!" Dan says.

The guy frowns.

I nudge Dan harder. To the guy, I offer, "How about eighty?"

For a long moment, the guy doesn't budge. Then he huffs, "Fine."

The man zips the case shut again and moves it behind the counter. I wait while he counts the cash and hands it to me. He also has me write my name and address in a ledger, where other people have noted the instruments they've sold to him. I glance at earlier pages but don't see anything for the sale of the rebab. The thief must have gotten out of writing down his information, somehow.

I add the money to my makeshift ziplock wallet. Three hundred sixty dollars! Over halfway there!

Clearing my throat, I ask, "So, could I see the rebab again, before I go?"

"Sure. It's in the back room." He rises with a sigh and goes to a door at the end of the room. When he returns, he has the rebab in his hand.

My heart tightens at the sight. This time when I reach for it, he does not stop me—though he watches with a wary gaze, as if I might run away with it in hand.

The nerves in my stomach melt away. The mulberry wood knows my fingers, and when I gently lift the body into my arms, it seems to warm against my skin. Wholeness shines in the mother-of-pearl designs, bright even in the artificial light of the shop, and sways in the beaded tassel my grandmother made. It makes vivid my mor jani's flash of a smile and my plar jan's steady hand on my shoulder. It flows in the blood of my ancestors, the Pashtuns who played this instrument before me.

I run my thumb over the strings, and though they've become terribly out of tune, the thrum of them between my palm and the goatskin base makes my whole body relax, almost as if a loved one were squeezing me into a hug.

"Whoa," Dan says as he leans closer to study the pegs. "So this came all the way from Afghanistan?"

I nod, too full of the feeling of it against my chest and in my arms to speak. If Baba could have this—if he could hold it again—he would be better. His heart would mend. Mine is growing stronger, just for these few seconds.

"That's so cool. Can you play it?"

"I'd need to tune it first." I glance at the shop owner.

He shrugs. "Just don't break the strings."

Hardly believing my luck, I move to one wall and sit on the floor, my feet tucked under my legs. Dan sits beside me to watch while I adjust the pegs, testing each string with several flicks. My ears remember the purity of the notes, remember the tones I need, without my trying to recall. This is not a foreign language I strive to master.

This is my mother tongue.

When the notes hit the right pitches, I stop tuning. I strum through snatches of songs, searching for one to make my *before* home more vibrant than the *after*. I haven't felt this way in weeks—I've been so worried about Baba and negotiating the trades. Now I feel a settling, like dust floating through light. A slow, drifting fall into rest.

Starting in the quiet deep inside me and flowing to my fingers, the song I want, the rhythm, emerges. My hands have lost much of their calluses, and the strings bite into my fingertips as I play the hard, quick notes. But if the rebab were mine now, today, I would play until my fingers bled. Play until I couldn't play anymore.

The other, better time presses up inside my head, pulling me across oceans and deserts and seasons and years and deaths to the house in Kandahar. To my mor jani's red-hennaed hands held out to me. To my plar jan's desk stacked with books and the sound of the lines he would read to us. The music pours out of me, first as pain, then as delight as the notes free my spirit.

The ringing of the door snaps me back to the shop in Cambridge. A new customer has entered, and seeing the unfamiliar face makes my fingers falter. The last note from the rebab fades away.

Dan applauds. "That. Was. *Awesome!*" he shouts.

"Your hands were almost smoking, you were moving so fast. You were like—" He mimics my playing, though it looks more like he's strumming an invisible electric guitar. "And then you were like—" He scrunches his face and makes his hands shake so quickly they're a blur. Then he stops, grinning. "That was wicked."

I can't help laughing a little. "Thanks?"

I glance toward the shop owner. Maybe seeing me and the rebab—seeing what it does when I hold it—changed his mind. But he's reading his magazine and only mumbles a greeting to the other customer.

Dan follows my gaze and spots the clock behind the counter. "Oh, jeez, it's four thirty already," he says, scrambling up. "We'd better get moving if we're going to beat the rush-hour crazies."

I get to my feet. When I put the rebab on the counter, I feel a tearing pain in my gut. How can I leave it? It's like leaving my heart.

I have to get the money—somehow I *will* get the money. I have six more days. Only a little less than a week.

"I'll be back," I say, partially to the rebab and partially to the owner. "I'll be back soon."

"Okay," the owner states, unaffected. He leans the rebab against the wall.

I swallow and turn away. The walk to the door stretches on and on. Is he taking care of the rebab? Is he protecting it from moisture? Is he keeping it somewhere warm so the goatskin won't stretch?

I have $360 in my wallet, $340 left to go. The next step is the laptop. Can I make $340 with that trade?

"That was seriously cool." Dan bounds out of the shop and turns around to face me while he walks backward. "I totally see why you want it back."

I start walking toward the T stop. Dan has no idea. With the rebab, all things are possible. Without it, I'm not sure anything is. "I *have* to get it back," I say, more to myself than to Dan.

But he's right beside me, so quick I didn't hear him coming. He throws his arm around my shoulder. "Nope," he says, his voice full of his boundless energy. "*We'll* get it back."

TRADE LOG

Days: 6
Have: $360
Need: $340

THINGS TO TRADE:

Laptop—now listed on eBay! (Layla's dad?)

COMPLETED TRADES:

1. Manchester United key chain -> iPod
2. Coins -> *Game Informer* magazines
3. iPod -> Figurines
4. Figurines -> $145
5. Magazines -> Combat boots
6. Story -> $50 + textbooks
7. Combat boots -> Art supplies
8. Art supplies -> Guitar
9. Textbooks -> $205
10. Guitar -> $80

23

WHEN WE ARRIVE AT ROXBURY CROSSING, DAN TAKES off for his house while I head the other direction to my apartment. My phone shows two missed calls, but I ignore them for a moment while I text Layla. *Thank you for the invitation. I would like to come! I need to check with Baba.*

I figure that if it's upsetting to Baba, I could still possibly excuse myself. Because not only do I want to go, I need to, for the laptop trade.

Right after I send the message, my phone starts to ring. It's Baba's number. I move my thumb over the answer button, but the call ends before I click.

Weird. I glance up.

Baba is walking toward me.

A startled guilt heats my face. Why is he here? He normally works until six or later. Why isn't he at the restaurant?

Perhaps he didn't notice me coming out of the T stop. Perhaps he thinks I'm coming home from the rec center.

But he's almost to me, and he's frowning.

"Where were you, Sami?" Baba demands in Pashto. He glances from me to Roxbury Crossing. "I've just come from the rec center. They told me you haven't been there all afternoon."

I stick my hands in my pockets and try to keep my tone light when I answer, hoping maybe he won't prod too much. "I was hanging out with Dan."

Baba fixes me in a hard stare. "And do you not have a phone to tell me where you are? I called twice before I saw you! Do you not have the respect to save your grandfather from concern?" His voice rises. "Do you know how I worried—realizing you weren't at the rec center? How was I meant to know what had happened to you?"

I duck my head. "I'm sorry—I wasn't thinking."

"You *were* thinking," he snaps. "You just were not thinking of family."

I want to sink into my shoes. I wish I were one of the squashed pieces of gum on the sidewalk. I wish I were invisible.

Baba rubs his face. "Sami, why are you hiding from me?"

I can't tell him. If I tell him, everything unravels—it

won't be a surprise or a gift, it will just be a silly-sounding plan. And he'll try to buy the rebab back himself, when *I'm* the one who lost the rebab in the first place. As much as I want to tell him, I'm too far into my trades to reveal the truth.

My phone dings before I find an answer. I reach for it out of habit. Baba sighs.

It's a text from Layla: *YES! If you take the T, we can meet you at a station near the river. I'll ask my parents which. Does your grandpa want to come? It'll probably be like 6-11 PM or later.*

"Who is your text from?" Baba asks.

"Layla." Before I say more, I hesitate. I need to ask permission, but it's not a good time. Baba's already mad at me. So instead of the question I want to ask, I say, "Why are you not at work?"

Baba hesitates, and his eyes shift away. He takes his white taqiyah off his head and pats it with his hand, all while studying the traffic and not looking at me.

Alarm hitches my breath. "Baba?"

"Apparently I am not a good dishwasher," he says abruptly. "I rest too often. I tell them it is for the dizziness, but they do not care about such things." He shrugs. "Perhaps I can find another job. One of the employees said they know someone like me who works as a janitor.

He used to be the chef to the American ambassador in Kabul, but now he vacuums hotel room floors. I could do such work."

"They fired you?" The very thought of someone dismissing my baba—the man crowds would gather to hear, whose hands are too precious to be wasted in bloodying soap—makes my body burn. "Are they allowed to do that?"

He waves me away and begins to walk. He looks smaller. Frailer. Old. "It is their decision. It is their business. They must choose what is right for them. Khuday Pak mehriban dey."

God is kind.

Though he acts calm, the disappointment lingers in his expression, and I feel like I can see the slow dying of his spirit.

We turn down our street and walk toward the apartment. My phone dings again, twice in a row.

The first is Dan: *Sent the laptop specs to Layla! OPERATION LAPTOP TRADE IS A GO.*

The second is Layla: *Did you ask? Are you coming?*

I glance at Baba, but the confidence I felt at the music shop is fading. I have to get the rebab back, and this is my absolute last chance to make the final trade. I have to take it.

I follow Baba into the apartment, and we slip off our

shoes by the door. The air is beginning to smell less like the old renters' cigarette smoke and more like spices and chai. I move a few steps, steel myself, and face Baba.

"I would like to go to the Fourth of July celebration," I say, all in a rush. "Layla's family offered to take me, and Dan's going, too. I think it's important for me to be there—it's an American tradition."

Baba still stands by the door. He says nothing, but his jaw tightens.

I hesitate. "It's from six to eleven at night. You're invited, too."

"No." Baba flips the lock shut and sets the keys on the kitchen counter. "After today? No. You need to spend more time at home, and the Fourth may well be the day before the end of Ramadan. You should be reflecting on the coming of Eid al-Fitr, not running around all night."

"But this is *important*."

"More important than your faith, your family?" Baba shakes his head. "No. No, I will not have you leave. It isn't a good idea. This is a time for us to be together. They will be busy with their own celebrations of their own nation."

"It's *our* nation, too, now," I snap. "I am only trying to get used to it—and you should be as well. Isn't that what you want? Isn't that what we've wanted all these years—a new home?"

"Not if it means forgetting the old one," he says heatedly.

I flinch as if he'd struck me. His face softens, and he reaches for me, but I back away.

"Sami, what am I to think?" Baba asks, his voice hopeless. "How am I to know what to do when you will not talk to me? When you turn to strangers for comfort instead of your family? What am I to think when you do not speak of the past anymore?"

I'm always thinking of the past! I want to shout. The guilt in my chest turns to anger. *I'm trying to remember! I'm trying to move forward!*

But my mouth is dry, and I can no longer feel the rebab's strings under my fingers. I am alone. Even here, even with Baba.

"Sami, tell me your heart," Baba says, almost a plea. "We are all we have."

I'm shaking my head. I'm saying words I don't mean, and I don't know why.

"No," I say, voice choked and hoarse. "No, *I* am all *you* have. But *I* have others now."

Horrified at my own words, I flee before Baba can say anything, before I can look at him.

I run into the bathroom and slam the door shut, locking it behind me. Then I sit in the tub and tug the curtain closed.

I hug my knees and wait for him to knock or shout or do anything. But he doesn't. The whole apartment is silent except for the pounding of my pulse.

My phone buzzes. It's Layla again. *Well???*

Blinking a haze out of my eyes, I type my response with one finger, one letter at a time.

I will come. Baba can't.

I tap send. Then I press my face against my knees.

24

IT'S THE FOURTH OF JULY, AND I'M DOING MY BEST TO focus on my goal: trading the laptop.

I'm doing my best *not* to think about how tonight Baba will be alone in the apartment, waiting for iftar to end today's fast all by himself.

We have barely exchanged words since our fight. When I stand by the door and break the quiet, it is like taking a hammer to stone. "I'm going," I say. Not a question.

Baba does not answer. He just sits there on the toshak, his prayer beads in hand. It's like he's turning into a shadow.

"Well, bye," I say, still standing there, waiting for a reaction.

"Be safe," Baba murmurs, so soft I almost don't hear it.

I nod and leave. He hadn't insisted I stay, and his words of parting might even be considered permission. But the whole walk to the T, I feel like I am dragging my feet through deep sand.

I can't stop thinking about Baba, even when I meet up with Dan and we catch our train.

"Come on—this is our stop," Dan says, tugging my sleeve when the doors open. He jumps the gap between the train and platform.

I force myself to think about the trade. And I hurry after him.

We have to work hard to stay together in the crowded press of people all going the same way. Dan mutters impatiently, but I find it comforting. It is familiar, if nothing else. I know crowds—crowds of chatter and dust in the markets around Afghanistan and Greece and Turkey. Crowds can be dangerous. They were at home, and even here a crowd is what got the rebab stolen. But crowds make me feel invisible and protected by the bodies around me—even if they're the bodies of sweaty and loud Americans.

We finally push through the turnstiles, and I see Layla and her family standing just outside the exit. She hops and shouts, "Sami! Sami! Dan! Sami! Dan!"

Dan looks around in the opposite direction, oblivious.

I grab his shirt and turn him the right way, and we both head toward them. A tall man has Jared in a sort of baby-carrier backpack, and Mrs. Michele grins while she picks up a huge bag full of food and blankets. Two older boys are bent over a phone together, apparently playing a game.

"Hey, Dan, Sami," Mrs. Michele says. "Thanks for meeting us here. This is Micah and Alex, Layla's older brothers. And my husband, Ty."

"Good to meet you." Mr. Ty grins. When Mrs. Michele isn't looking, he nods toward my heavy backpack and gives me a subtle thumbs-up. A knot of nerves settles in my stomach. I want to get the trade over with—prove to myself that I made the right decision in coming. But it's not time. We need a moment without Mrs. Michele around.

"Hey," says the oldest son, glancing up for two seconds.

"Hi," says the other.

Mr. Ty nudges Micah's shoulder. "Come on. Put that away. Let's get moving before all the decent places are taken. Stay close!"

Layla sticks beside me and Dan while her parents lead the way, her brothers just behind them. "We aren't going to the Oval, where the band plays. They have too many restrictions on stuff, plus we would have had to get here at like seven this morning to snag a good spot. We'll find a place by the sailing pavilion and still be able to hear most of the music over the water and on the speakers."

"Works for me," Dan says.

"The concert starts at eight thirty," she goes on, "and then fireworks at ten thirty. Until then, there's plenty to do. We brought a beach ball, and my mom brought some hot dogs and burgers. You can do burgers, right, Sami? She made sure they're halal."

"Yeah, that's fine." I nod. "I just have to wait until sunset."

"Right. That's okay—but Jared will have to eat earlier."

"Oh—you don't have to wait for me to have dinner." I edge around a couple too busy taking pictures to notice they are blocking the way. "I don't mind—I'm used to it."

"You sure?" she asks. She looks a lot like her mom when she makes that worried expression.

"Definitely."

"*Good*, because I'm *starving*," Dan cuts in, rubbing his stomach.

Layla rolls her eyes.

The whole park is covered by people—on blankets,

in chairs, or just sitting on the grass. Someone is playing loud music on a speaker. I've heard the singer before— he seems to be the same one who's always singing the type of song with long, low words that slur between notes.

"Is this Garth Brooks?" I ask Layla.

Dan turns to stare at me. "Um. *No.* It's Rascal Flatts."

Layla giggles. "Hey, they're both country singers. He was close."

"There's more than one?" I feel sort of stupid. "I knew there was a woman and a man . . ."

Dan groans.

"He's not wrong," Layla puts in, elbowing Dan. "They all sound the same."

Dan puts a hand against his forehead. "*Never* let my mom hear you say that."

We find an empty stretch of grass along the Charles River, and Mr. Ty lays out a picnic blanket. Mrs. Michele helps smooth it out, and Layla's brothers run off to some of their friends.

Mrs. Michele sits and opens the cooler. I barely hold in a sigh, taking a seat myself. The trade isn't going to happen right away, it's clear. The knot in my stomach just gets tighter and tighter.

"I'll distract her," Layla whispers, sitting beside me. She lifts her hand to wave. "Mrs. Johnson is over there, and once they get talking, they'll never stop."

Mrs. Johnson—a round-faced woman with curly hair—spots Layla and breaks into a grin. She comes over and calls, "Michele! How are you?"

Mrs. Michele gets to her feet, and the two hug. I glance aside at Mr. Ty, and he nods, reaching for his wallet. While the women talk, I push my backpack closer to Mr. Ty's bag.

But suddenly a piece of their conversation breaks through my focus.

"Are you all going to do anything? Are there any presents you really want?"

"We'll probably go out to dinner." Mrs. Michele offers Mrs. Johnson a Coke. "And . . . I think what I want most would be for the boys to clean their rooms. Or maybe a new kettle . . ."

I freeze. Layla casts me an uncertain look.

Mr. Ty turns to the women. "And a laptop, right?"

"Oh!" Mrs. Michele smiles. "I forgot to tell you. I found a laptop today on Craigslist. It was a great deal, so I snatched it up!"

"Happy birthday to you," Mrs. Johnson says with a laugh.

"What?" Layla exclaims.

Dan just gapes.

"Oh!" Mr. Ty forces a smile. "That's great!"

My whole chest starts hurting.

"Yep," Mrs. Michele says. "It's really nice. I'll show it to you when we get home." Turning back to Mrs. Johnson, she asks about something to do with children. The words stop translating in my head.

While she's distracted, Layla and Mr. Ty lean over to me.

Layla whispers something, but I have to concentrate to understand. ". . . *so* sorry."

"I had no idea she was planning to do this," Mr. Ty adds. I feel his gaze studying me, but I can't look at any of them.

"It's okay." My voice says the words, but my lungs don't want to fill with air. I rock to my feet—I have to get away from his concern and Dan's frustration and Layla's embarrassment. "It's fine, really. I'm—ah—just going to walk around a little bit."

I leave before they can answer. My mind turns circles, unwilling to accept this. I've come so far only to make a bad calculation on the trade I needed the most. I feel worse than I did with the first trade for the broken iPod. Not only do I still need $340—I used up $120 to buy the laptop and the battery, and that's money I can't get back.

Sneakers smack on the pavement behind me. "Sami—" Layla touches my elbow.

Dan comes to my other side. "You okay?"

"Yeah." I'm desperate to hide my disappointment. It wasn't Layla's fault, or Mr. Ty's—I'm the one who made this mess. I try to breathe deeply. My body feels like it's sinking into cold water. Instead of looking at them, I search our surroundings. "Hey, what's that woman giving away?"

"Glow sticks. We should get some." Layla's voice sounds about as falsely happy as mine, but as long as we're both pretending, it doesn't have to be so bad.

"It's not the end of the world," Dan says suddenly. "So Layla's dad can't buy the laptop now. We just need to find someone else. I mean, we can list *ours* on Craigslist."

"Sometimes listings on there are really funny," Layla adds. "We could do something to make ours stand out . . . like, write it from the computer's perspective!"

"I am computer," Dan says in a robotic voice. "I need home."

Layla laughs.

They keep spouting ideas while we get a few glow sticks. Layla shows me how to crack the tube to make it change from a muted color to a bright neon. She only does one, though, because she says the glow might fade out before it's dark. I nod. Even though we have a new plan, my insides still feel like they're drowning.

I wave the glow stick and force myself to smile.

"We're going to sell the laptop, Sami," Layla says.

"Yeah," I reply, trying to make it sound like I actually agree. "It'll all work out."

But I have no idea how.

25

"ALMOST TIME FOR FIREWORKS!" LAYLA SAYS, CHECKING her phone and then rubbing her hands together. "Have you ever seen fireworks before, Sami?"

"Some." In Turkey, they set off small batches around New Year's, but normally Baba took me out of the city. He didn't like them. And I've seen the ones that spark when they're thrown on the ground. Sometimes kids use them on the street, and they remind me of gunshots. It always makes my heart pound.

I glance at the barges on the river. I was thinking so much about the laptop trade, I hadn't really thought about the fireworks.

"Well, these are awesome," Dan assures me. "Best in the country, I bet."

Mr. Ty pulls Jared into his lap. "Do you hear that, bud? Almost time for fireworks."

Mrs. Michele dumps the last of our trash from dinner into a bag, then leans over. "It's going to be loud, but you have nothing to be afraid of. And they'll be so bright!"

Jared sucks his fist. He doesn't seem worried.

I rub the scar on my arm, trying to ignore my churning stomach. How loud do they mean? But I'm too embarrassed to ask. It should be fine. I'm in America. I'm with my friends. I'm safe.

Anyway, there are so many people here to celebrate. They all look happy, with their faces painted blue and red and white and their T-shirts covered in patriotic messages. More people have come since we arrived. Lots more. They are pressing up against the sidewalk and overflowing into the grass behind it. The mass of voices rises, forceful and clamorous, competing to be heard above the music. A policeman wanders down the path, waving to people and smiling at kids. He has a gun in the holster at his hip.

Plenty of Americans have guns, right? How many might be carrying them now?

It's a warm evening, so most people are wearing clothes that wouldn't hide a gun. I search the crowd. No one in my view seems to have one.

"My favorite part is in the beginning," Layla's telling Dan. "They do a lot of those weeping-willowy ones then."

"Pfft, boring." He rocks back. The glow sticks looped around his neck cast his face in a strange green light. "I like the end, where they all come at once!"

A toddler somewhere starts to cry. The loudspeakers announce that it's almost time. I shift on my legs, trying to get comfortable. The man in front of us is wearing a jacket, and he pushes it out of the way to scratch his ribs. I don't see a holster on him, either. But maybe the other side?

I try to breathe through my nose. Everything's fine. I don't know why I'm even noticing all these things.

"Pay attention, Sami," Layla says, glancing over her shoulder with a grin. "You have to tell us which are *your* favorites once it's done."

I nod, forcing a smile. "Okay."

The couple to my left bursts into laughter, and I jump. Everyone around me is so happy—even Layla and Dan. It's like they think no one could ever hurt them.

It makes my eyes sting. I'm not sad, but my eyes are burning, and air hitches in my lungs.

Hot-dog smell mixed with Mrs. Michele's perfume and the sour hint of beer all turn to gunk in my throat. The music crackling on the speakers gets louder as other people snap off their own radios. I breathe in through my nose and exhale through my mouth.

"Okay, folks," the announcer says, "count down with me! Five . . ."

I'm becoming weightless, lifting above my body.

The people join in to shout, "Four . . ."

It's like I'm looking down at the crowd, down at myself, sitting with hands clenched on top of my knees.

"Three . . . !"

Four policemen stand together, staring toward the river.

"Two!"

Mr. Ty covers Jared's ears. The other toddler still screams.

"ONE!"

The music swells. A rocket booms into the sky, trailed by glimmering sparks, and my spirit falls as it lifts.

The sky explodes. I land in my body.

Every nerve is wrong. *Everything* is wrong. I flatten to the ground. Hands over my head. The explosion shakes the grass. Body. Bone. I grab for Dan, Layla. *Get down*, I want to say. *Get—*

But they're laughing. Pointing. The light of the fireworks illuminates the faces in the crowd. Bright eyes turned skyward. White teeth gleaming. Smiling. Everyone's smiling. Their shirts are red. The woman to my left turns, slow, to frown at me. Her silver earrings flash.

The leaves in the tree above us rustle. Blocks away, a dog barks. Once, twice, three times. The air smells like smoke. Sharp smoke. Gunpowder.

Someone touches my shoulder—Mrs. Michele. She's leaning into my vision. I can't hear her speak, but I read her lips. "You okay?"

I nod. My limbs are connected wrong. They jerk and shudder when I push myself up. Sweat drips down my neck. Everything's slow, when I know it can't really be going at this speed. Dan's shirt has a tiny hole right above his shoulder. Layla's beads jingle as she tilts her head back. I am paralyzed.

Another firework whistles into the air.

I close my eyes, but the sound hits me like a force. It crackles in my chest. Lodges there. Rattles my ribs. I can't breathe. I can't.

They don't know. They don't know we're under attack. I'm the only one. I have to warn them. I can't open my mouth. I can't breathe. It's wrong, it's wrong, it's *wrong*.

My eyes shut tight, I fight to unlock my jaw. The crowd rises in a cheer, and the music lifts with the orchestra in full force. This isn't Afghanistan. This is America. I'm *fine*. I'm *safe*.

Safe, safe, safe. Over and over. Keep thinking it. *Safe, safe, safe.*

Air trickles into my lungs. I try to make them expand. Gunpowder—I taste it on my tongue, lightly, only a hint. Metallic. Burning.

If I make myself watch the fireworks, from launch to explosion, my body will understand. They're only shooting into the sky. Not hurting anything. I shouldn't be like this. No one else is like this.

I peel my eyes open. One and then the other.

Two points of light shoot off the barges, sputtering into the gray-smoke remains of the others. They blip out for a second. The music changes key.

The fireworks burst into color—both red and blooming. Their combined roar hits my heart like a punch. I breathe in puffed chokes.

This is the last feeling my mor had as all the blood left her body. This is the last thing my plar heard.

The wedding—
Baba reaching for me—
"Come down—"
Shattered windows—
"Come down—"

Five bright lights streak into the sky with a shrill scream. Layla covers her ears. Dan laughs at her. I push myself back. Rock to the balls of my feet. Crouch.

They explode—each of them spinning into five

different, smaller explosions. My stomach heaves. All I have eaten rises in my throat.

"Sami?" Mrs. Michele asks.

Dan and Layla turn toward me.

But I run.

My shoe slides on someone's picnic blanket. Rasps over the pavement.

Boom rips through the air and hits my back. I stumble, scrape my palm. Run harder.

The policemen notice me. One opens his mouth. My head is full of the pounding music and shouting crowd. Each step lands heavy, jolts up my ankles and legs. Cold sweat drips off my nose.

"Come down—" Baba reaches for me. "Come down—"

Glass shattered across the courtyard.

"Come down—

"We have to run—"

The memory twists me, tunes me, plays me. I shove past people on the street corner. My gasped breaths burn. No matter how far I run, I can't stop seeing the wedding.

26

WE ARE AT THE WEDDING. BABA IS FINISHING A SOLO on his rebab. I lean against my plar, and he puts an arm around my shoulders while he laughs at a comment his friend made. His chest bounces against my back. Across the the melman khana, the guest room, my mor jani has her chin in her hands, eyes closed as she listens. Today she only wears the large porlaney scarf, wrapped over her hair and draped across her chest.

Other women move between the low tables, serving tea and treats. My many cousins are scattered around, entertaining themselves or watching Baba. One of my aunts, the mother of the newly married husband, flits between the kitchen and this room, taking obvious pride in how many family members she is able to host in her home. Out of the dozens here, there are only a few I do not recognize.

I am eight years old. It has been a long wedding ceremony, and I am bored.

As Baba finishes his solo, I nudge my plar's arm. "Plar," I say when he looks down, "did you see the grapes in the courtyard?"

"The trellis?" he asks, the laugh lingering in his voice. "I do not know if the grapes are ripe yet, Sami jan."

"I'll find out! Can I go outside?" I try to make my eyes bigger, pleading. "Only for a few minutes!"

"What's this?" Baba comes toward us, the rebab still in his arms. "Have I bored my poor grandson beyond bearing?"

"No, I believe it's only love that has bored him." Plar smiles and shifts to his feet. "Come, I'll go with you."

"I can go myself," I object, annoyed.

Plar shakes his head. "Perhaps if you can interest your cousins, you could go together. But I don't want you to be alone. Come, don't you want to see how many grapes you can find?"

"Not with his father, perhaps," Baba says. He shifts the rebab and offers me his right hand. "We will bring our treasures back from the hunt."

"Yes!" I take Baba's hand. "Plar, you can come when I gather enough for you and Mor."

"Very well." Plar pats my head. "Your mor and I will come when you are ready."

"Let's go!" Now that I've decided, I'm impatient to leave. I all but drag Baba toward the door, even though he tries to give the rebab to my plar. "Come, come! You can play, and maybe then my boring cousins will join us!"

"Very well, O Determined One." Baba laughs and doesn't bother to put the rebab down.

I wave toward Mor jani, and she lifts her chin off her hands to grin.

Baba and I leave together.

I do not look back.

I do not look back.

I run ahead into the warm sunlight, pausing by the door to slip on my sandals. There are so many pairs, it takes me some searching to find them. But finally I am free, dashing out the door and around the outside kitchen.

The day is late, and the wedding will go for many more hours. Between me and the high wall of the compound is a tall trellis of woven wood. Grape vines are twined through the gaps, their green leaves almost covering the skeleton structure. I spot a bunch of green grapes farther up. Looping my arm around one of the poles, I start to climb. The trellis stays sturdy under my weight.

Baba, meanwhile, has set his rebab against the wooden frame. He holds his hands near my back. "I'll catch you if you fall. Go on."

I reach for the top beam. Dust falls from the leaves

onto my head. With my feet, I nudge the vines aside until I'm sure I can swing up and stand without crushing them.

The first bunch of grapes are not ripe, but I find better ones hidden under the leaves. I pass them down to Baba until we have gathered two handfuls.

"Come, Sami. We should return. This is plenty of harvest."

"But I've just found more," I say, stretching my tired hands and crawling farther along the length of the vines. The far side of the trellis has grapes tinted purple. I don't want to go inside again. "Get Plar and Mor! We can eat out here, and you can play. And tell Amina and Isa and Rashid and Navid and—"

Baba laughs. "Very well, just give me a moment to gather all your favorite cousins," he says. "I'll—"

The *crack* of tearing stone slices the air. The window glass shatters across the courtyard. Baba falls against the trellis, and it shudders. I freeze, pressed into the vines by the force. The roar keeps going in my head. My aunt's house is full of holes.

Baba looks from me to the building. He's covered in dust. He seems to move slowly. His face—mouth open, eyes wide—his face—

The screams begin.

The air smells like fire.

Baba lifts his arms to me. "Sami—"

The windows are empty.

Inside: *Patter, patter, patter.*

"Come down—"

Gunshots.

"Come down—"

My parents.

"We have to run—"

Glass covers the growing black-blue of the courtyard like shattered bits of night.

Baba grabs my ankle and tugs it free of the vines. I can't move myself. I let him pull me through the gaps in the structure. I slide into his arms.

When my feet touch earth, the numbness thaws. A strangled sound—more cry than language—rips in my throat, and I launch myself toward the house. Baba catches me by the shirt.

Patter, patter, patter.

"Sami," he says, gripping my shoulders and trying to hold me still. "Sami, no."

I shake my head. I have to go to them. There are still screams. They could be alive. They could—

"The blast came from the melman khana." Baba's eyes are red from smoke or tears, but he doesn't blink, doesn't look away from me. "You have to hide."

He wraps his arms around me and lifts. The rebab is

still sitting against the trellis. I grab it as we pass. Baba covers my head and folds me to his chest as he runs.

The house is between us and the gate to the street. *Patter, patter, patter,* go the guns in loud, sharp, short shots. Baba takes the four stairs two at a time and pushes open the door to the outhouse. There isn't much space, but he sets me on the dry mud ground away from the bare hole in the middle of the floor.

"Hide here," he says. He is Pashtun, and Pashtuns do not cower at a fight.

A woman's scream lifts above the noise. I grab Baba around the waist, bury my face against his fine wedding shirt, and hold on. I will not let him go. I cannot.

"Sami, I must—"

I grip the shirt in my fists. Hold.

"The others—"

I hold.

"My family—"

"I am your family," I gasp into his chest. "Stay. *Please.*"

His whole body shakes.

I hold.

We stay.

We stay in the dank, foul outhouse as the gunshots slowly stop.

Then the screams stop.

The entire complex is full of silence.

We stay.

Eventually vehicles drive up outside the wall. Their tires bang over the unpaved, uneven road. The gate groans open.

More explosions—smaller, but loud enough to shake the outhouse. I whimper, tightening my arms around Baba. There are five, and then the sound of boots.

"It's the police, Sami," Baba whispers, more exhausted than relieved. "It's the police."

Soon, they escort us out.

Smoke pours through the holes of the house like blood.

My mouth tastes like dust and gunpowder.

They take us to a safe place. They ask for our story. Baba talks. They tell us a suicide bomber detonated. Two others with AK-47s broke in during the confusion. They targeted the survivors. The bomber was a distant cousin, one I did not recognize. The Taliban have claimed the attack. They say there were Western supporters in the room.

A few people survived, we are told. An uncle, a cousin, two wives. Navid and three of my young cousins are rushed to the hospital. We do not know it then, but they will not live long.

My mor and plar—

They were gone hours before the police came.

The man who tells me this does it softly. Baba presses his face against my head.

"The blast shadow from the outdoor kitchen saved you both," the man says. "You are lucky you survived."

I sit, consumed by silence. After the blast, all noise has been slowly drained from my mind.

Lucky you survived.

The T train slows to a stop. The doors slide open, and the conductor mumbles, "Roxbury."

I lurch to my feet and stagger off. Drunk teenagers leer at me in passing, push me aside as they go to board. I drag myself up the stairs.

The memory runs through my mind again, like a film I can't turn off. I feel nothing now. I can only let it play as I walk down the streets, arms crossed tight over my middle. My phone is dinging. It has been for a while. I dig it out, shaking so hard I drop it once. Thankfully, the screen doesn't crack. *Baba wouldn't like that.* The thought is wrong, tiny, strange.

The memory plays while I check the missed texts and calls from Dan and Layla and Layla's parents. I open one text from Dan. My fingers jitter so much as I type my reply that it's only because of autocorrect that the message is legible.

Got sick. Am home. Fine.

Send. Then I turn off my phone.

Somehow I arrive at the apartment. I unlock the door. Baba is sitting on one of the toshaks, thumbing through his prayer beads. He lifts his head when I come in.

"Sami?"

I stagger to the wall and sink down on the toshak beside him. My whole body is shaking. "I'm sorry," I gasp. "I'm sorry."

"Sami?" he asks, touching my forehead. "Is it the memories?"

"I'm sorry. I'm sorry for leaving." I try to gulp air. Even while I talk, the memories repeat and repeat. They run and run and run. My plar laughs and my mor smiles and the windows crack, burst. "I'm sorry for leaving."

Baba reaches for me. "Sami."

"I *hate* this!" I shout, pressing the palms of my hands against my closed eyes. "I hate being lucky. I hate surviving! I *hate it*!"

Baba brushes a hand through my hair. "I know," he whispers. "I know."

"I'm not strong!" My voice squeaks into tonelessness.

"I'm not brave! Everyone says survivors are, but I'm *not*. This doesn't feel like surviving—it feels like torture."

I try to breathe, and still the memories run. Somewhere in the distance, fireworks explode. I can't help flinching, hating a world where explosions are entertainment.

"I would not wish this on my enemy, let alone you, the son of my son," Baba says softly. "Do you know how many times I have longed to return to the hours before—the minutes before?"

I look at him. The memories keep playing.

Baba's face is lined, but he meets my gaze directly. "It is a torture to go on," he says. "It is, Sami."

"Then why do it?"

He is quiet a long time. My head hurts, but I keep watching him. Right now, I'm not sure anything is worth this.

Finally, he whispers, "Because *we* survived. I must live for you, and you must live for me. Our loss brings us urgency, compassion. We live for each other and the others who are hurting. This may yet bring us healing. And even if it doesn't"—he presses a kiss to my forehead—"I will be with you, and you with me."

"But you won't," I blurt, eyes stinging. "You won't always be with me."

In movies or stories, this is the part where he would

tap my heart and say, *I will always be here.* He doesn't, though. Memory is never the same as living. I know this well. My parents will never be alive again, no matter how hard I try to remember, no matter how much I hold them in my heart. They loved me, and I love them still, but they are gone.

I left them. They left me.

"I may not always be with you," Baba says, "but God will give you others. Sergeant Pyciors to help you on your journey. Dans to welcome you. Laylas to encourage you. And many more we don't know yet."

"It isn't the same." I lower my gaze to the carpet.

"No," he agrees. "There are no replacements for the ones we lose. But there are abundant additions."

I think of Peter and the team. Of how he felt replaced, even when I tried to include him. Of how he attacked instead of accepting the change.

"If we allow it, God will gather others around us, and we will not be left alone." Baba shifts, exhaling. "I must be honest with you—I do not know if it ever will truly stop hurting. But it will not always be *this* way, Sami jan."

He draws me to lean on him, his arm around me. He smells like chai and soap. I breathe it in, my lungs hiccupping, and my bones still shuddering.

"Now rest here and close your eyes." He rubs my

shoulder. "Try to be comfortable. And I will be right here, with you, should you need anything."

My eyes close. The images continue—Plar's laughter and the force of the blast and the pattern of gunshots.

Baba murmurs, "I will do my very best to not leave you."

"I know," I whisper.

"Khuday Pak mehriban dey." He says the familiar phrase, the one we Afghans exchange whenever something terrible happens. "God is kind. We are like mountain soil after a fire. Hope is born in that soil."

My head burns with the memories. I long for a time of hope.

With the smell of spices in the room, and the carpet fibers scratching against my feet, and the gentle rhythm of Baba's heartbeat under my head, somehow—despite everything—I fall asleep.

27

I WAKE WITH A THROBBING HEADACHE. STIFF AND TIRED, I turn on my phone to check the time. It's already noon.

For a moment, I stare at the screen, unable to understand it. I've *never* slept in this late. I feel heavy, like my brain is full of scratchy wool.

Two voice mails and fourteen missed texts flash on the screen. Most are from Dan. I scroll through them, too groggy to really care. The first couple are from last night:

Hope you got home okay. The finale was cool!

I think I had too much sugar, LOL. Still awake!!! Are you?

You going to go to the rec center tomorrow? Lots of us are!

You should COMMMME!

The next are from this morning:

RISE AND SHINE! I'm going to the rec center. You should come!

I'm here!!! Are you coming?

Coach and Juniper are dating! SO WEIRD!

I just totally kicked Benj's butt! You need to be here!

We're going to get lunch at McDonald's and play some more games. COME!!!

?????

Are you alive????

I click through Layla's three messages—two asking if I'm all right and one inviting me to the lunch with the others. Then I toss my phone aside. I don't feel like answering.

Today is the deadline. I only have $360 saved. It's not enough. I can't believe I was so stupid about the laptop.

Maybe the rebab won't sell the instant it's put on sale. That's likely. But how am I going to come up with $340 when I'm competing against all of Cambridge? All of the internet, for that matter, if he puts the ad up on eBay. The more I try to think of options and possibilities, the more my head hurts. I find myself just staring at the ceiling.

My stomach cramps, like it wants to remind me

it's still Ramadan. I'm hungry enough to eat a whole lamb.

Baba cracks open the bedroom door. "You're awake—that's promising," he says, leaning on the wall. He points to folded clothes beside my bed. "Get dressed and wash. They've officially announced the sixth is Eid, so I thought you could use one of your presents a day early."

Baba leaves the room. I prop myself on my elbow. On top of my neatly folded old jeans and socks is a new, secondhand Manchester United T-shirt—a little thin and well worn. The heaviness in my head settles on my shoulders.

At home in Afghanistan, we used to spend the whole week preparing for Eid. It was the busiest time at the bazaars. Plar would take me to find new clothes to wear for the holiday, and we would pick out a shalwar kameez for him and a collarless one for Baba. The morning of Eid al-Fitr, we'd celebrate with gift giving, music, and a breakfast of roht. My mor could never make it without burning the top. I miss the taste of slightly charred sugar.

Later in the day, my cousins would come, crowding into our house, excited about gifts of money from the adults. They would sing, "Eidie, eidie!"

I gather the clothes. Baba must have had to save so much to afford the shirt.

And I didn't get him the rebab.

Just to make myself more miserable, I look at my record one more time. I skip down to the trade list itself, ignoring my other notes.

COMPLETED TRADES:
1. Manchester United key chain -> iPod
2. Coins -> *Game Informer* magazines
3. iPod -> Figurines
4. Figurines -> $145
5. Magazines -> Combat boots
6. Story -> $50 + textbooks
7. Combat boots -> Art supplies
8. Art supplies -> Guitar
9. Textbooks -> $205
10. Guitar -> $80

Pushing back a sigh, I slip into the bathroom. I wash my face first, trying to wipe away the lingering shame from last night, and then get dressed. My old jeans have shortened, or I've grown in the past month, because the hem hits above my ankle. It isn't hard to guess that I'll wake up to new trousers tomorrow, which only makes me feel more guilty.

When I come out, Baba glances up from his work of tidying the living room. "It fits? Good."

"Thank you," I say, unable to look at him directly.

"You are very welcome. Come, sit and rest."

For a while, Baba plies me with questions about the rec center, about the team and my friends. It is more than he has tried to talk in the past month. I'm not sure if it is the spirit of Eid al-Fitr, or if he is trying to distract me from last night. I answer as much as I can, though it feels like talking through a fog. I'm numb and exhausted.

After an hour or two, I lie down in my room again. My mind keeps drifting to Eid. In Afghanistan, we would go home-to-home feasting. We would eat until we couldn't stand another swallow—and still we would eat more. It was my mor's favorite time of year—the only time when we could be fairly certain we would see a full day of peace.

My phone buzzes every twenty minutes or so, but I ignore it.

Perhaps the rebab is already placed in the shop window. Perhaps someone has already come to take it.

Baba looks in to check on me around four fifteen. "How are you, Sami?"

"I'm fine," I say, plucking at the carpet on the floor beside my mattress. My phone buzzes twice in a row.

"Is that one of your friends?" Baba asks.

I nod.

"Well, why don't you answer them?"

I sigh, but explaining that I can't find the will to

care about anything—not even soccer—sounds like too much work. Sitting up, I look at my notifications. I have a few dozen messages from Dan, but I only look at the last couple.

You need to come!!!!
The rec center is open late today!
We have a surprise for you!!!
Everyone wants to see you!
Be here by 5 OR ELSE.
If you don't come, I'm going to get you!
I know where you live!!
PLEASE COME???

"It's Dan," I tell Baba. "He wants me to come play soccer."

"Well, then why are you moping on your bed? Go and play."

I look at him, surprised. "But you wanted me to spend time with family."

Baba lifts his eyebrows. "And you are spending time with family by languishing in here?"

"Earlier—you hated when I went with them."

"I didn't hate it; I just wanted you to stop running from me. Friends bring hope, Sami jan. That is all I want for you—hope." He straightens from leaning on the doorframe and waves me out. "Have fun. I will prepare a big iftar meal for when you come home."

I hesitate still, part of me embarrassed to face Layla and Dan after my strangeness at the celebration. But I realize that this, like the shirt, is a gift Baba is giving me—the gift of letting me go.

So I rise and hug him. Then I pull on my shoes and jog down the hall and stairs to the street. It feels good to move.

I text Dan: *Coming*.

He answers seconds later: *YAAAASSSSSS!!!!!*

28

WHEN I GET TO THE REC CENTER, DAN AND LAYLA
are waiting outside. Dan runs over as soon as I come
through the gate, grinning so hard I can see almost all
his teeth. Layla dashes after him.

"*Finally!*" Dan exclaims. "Wait till you see—"

Layla smacks his arm. "Don't ruin it!" She grabs the
front of my shirt and hauls me toward the building.
"Come on!"

My face heats, but I go with them. I'm not sure I
actually have a choice. "What—?"

Miss Juniper isn't at the reception desk. Instead,
there's a little sign that says HEAD STRAIGHT BACK FOR
THE 5:00 EVENT. Layla releases my shirt and sprints forward, bounding into the gym a few seconds before Dan
and me. When the door swings open, my whole team is
there with a bunch of other people.

As soon as I step in, they shout, "Welcome to the auction!"

I blink at them, stunned and confused. On the far wall, there's a banner with handwritten letters on it that says LAPTOP AUCTION: BEST LAPTOP EVER. On either side of the words are elaborate geometric patterns. Someone's strung lights from the basketball net down to a table with a sleek black tablecloth. A box covered in shiny red fabric sits on the table, with the laptop Mr. Ty didn't buy displayed on the fancy silk. I forgot Dan and Layla had it after I left the fireworks.

"We decided to host an auction!" Dan tells me, pointing to the laptop. "Layla had the idea last night!"

"Hamida and I did the banner—she made the designs," Layla says. "We've been working on this all day!"

Layla turns me toward the gathering of people. They're all grinning at my surprise. "We invited all the team and their families and Coach invited his friends from Northeastern and Hamida told her uncle and he invited a bunch of people from Islamic Society of Boston."

Miss Juniper leans her shoulder against Coach's arm. I recognize some of the people from the mosque—the woman in a hijab who joked with me about the overpriced shop and others who always speak with Baba.

Mr. Farid is there, too, smiling. My brain hasn't caught up with what's going on. Mr. Lincoln raises his hand in a wave, and Miss Cheryl, his student assistant, beams beside him.

"I'm *super* excited for this, Sami," Miss Cheryl says. "Even the Geek Squad couldn't fix my old one."

"The Geek . . . ?" The words sound familiar, but I don't understand.

"Computer doctors," Mr. Lincoln explains.

"Come meet everyone," Layla says, grabbing my sleeve and pulling me forward.

Layla and Dan parade me around, introducing me to everyone's parents. A lot of them have heard of the trades through my teammates and wish me luck for today. Benj takes the hand of the old woman beside him and says, *"Este es Sami, mi amigo—el que me ayudó a conseguir el iPod."*

"Bueno, bueno! Estoy encantada de conocerte, Sami. Gracias por ayudar a mi nieto."

"She says hi," Benj translates, beaming. "And thanks for the iPod. See? My Spanish is better already."

Do all these people need a laptop? They're all talking and laughing and seem so happy to be at an auction. I introduce my friends from the mosque to Dan and Layla. Even though the gymnasium is huge, much bigger than this group of people, it feels full. I know almost every face—the only strangers are my teammates' family members. They're not all here to buy a laptop. They're here because they care about me.

"All right, everyone!" Coach says in his most coach voice. "Time for the auction! If you'll please gather by the laptop . . ."

Layla and Dan take me to the front and place me by the table. My neck gets hot. I'd rather be under the bleachers than in front of everyone.

Coach rolls up a *Game Informer* magazine and hits it on the tabletop like he's a judge. "Order, order!" he says, smiling. "First up, I'm going to let Dan say a few words about the laptop specs, and then we'll proceed with the moment you've all been waiting for: the auction!"

The audience cheers. Miss Juniper even cups her mouth and shouts, "Woo-hoo!"

Coach steps aside for Dan. He runs through the specs of the computer, most of which I don't understand. He explains the new laptop battery. Miss Cheryl and some others have questions, which he answers with confidence. When everyone seems satisfied, Coach takes his place by the table again.

My heart pounds. This is the eleventh trade. My laptop for at least $340, I hope.

Holding the rolled magazine up, Coach calls, "Okay, everyone, who will start us off with one hundred dollars?"

One of the Islamic Society of Boston members lifts his hand.

"One hundred dollars! One twenty-five?"

Miss Cheryl raises her hand.

"I've got one hundred twenty-five! Who will give me one fifty?"

Mr. Lincoln lifts his hand.

"Hey," Miss Cheryl protests, laughing.

"What?" Mr. Lincoln shrugs. "Just making this interesting."

"I see one fifty! How about one seventy-five?"

Miss Cheryl raises her hand again. "Here!"

"One hundred seventy-five! Two hundred?"

My breath sticks in my throat.

No one raises their hand at first, but then one of the parents waves.

"Two hundred!" Coach looks at Miss Cheryl. "Two fifty?"

She bites her lip.

"Two hundred fifty? Anyone?"

Mr. Lincoln takes out some cash and passes it to Miss Cheryl, and her hand shoots straight up.

"Two hundred fifty dollars, going once . . . twice . . ." Coach bangs the magazine on the table. "Sold to the lovely lady in the front!"

"Yes!" Miss Cheryl dashes forward and starts to count out twenties. The others begin to talk among themselves, and Dan, Layla, and Hamida run to join me at the front of the room.

"So?" Dan seems to be almost bursting out of his skin with excitement. "What's the total? How much do you have?"

I don't have to pull out my phone to know the answer. Two hundred fifty dollars for the laptop is not quite enough.

"With the laptop sale I have six hundred ten dollars," I say.

"Nooooo!!!" Dan groans.

"Hold on!" Hamida shushes him. "How much do you need?"

"Seven hundred," I tell her. "I just need ninety dollars more. Just another trade or two."

"Okay, let's think." Layla and Dan start talking over each other, throwing out ideas, but Hamida runs off across the gym. I rack my brain. What else do I have? What else can I trade or sell or do? Baba gave me this shirt, which means I could maybe trade an old one. Or my backpack—I won't need that for another few months now that school is over.

Hamida comes bouncing back toward us, Mr. Farid at her side. "Well done, Sami," he says.

I glance at Dan and Layla. "I didn't do much."

Layla rolls her eyes. Dan shakes his head.

"I think your friends might disagree." Mr. Farid smiles and takes an envelope out of his pocket. "I was saving this for Eid, but Hamida says I should give it to you now. Eid Mubarak, Sami."

"Eid Mubarak," I repeat, my hand closing around the envelope.

Dan taps my arm. "What's in it?"

Mr. Farid moves to speak with Coach, and I tear the paper open. When I slip out the card inside, a bunch of cash starts to fall free. Layla gasps, Hamida beams, and Dan catches the bills and starts counting.

My throat closes and my eyes sting. I have to work to make the words on the paper come into focus.

Sami,

So that our T stops may resound with songs of home, please accept this eidie a little early.

From,
Farid Wazir and Your Family
at the Islamic Cultural Center

P.S. When your grandfather has the
rebab again, have him talk to me—I think
I know some permanent gigs he could
play!

"Two hundred dollars!" Dan breathes, holding up the cash.

I'm paralyzed, caught somewhere between disbelief and joy and uncertainty. I don't have a right to this generosity—I deserve none of it.

"You d-didn't—" I stutter, my voice cracking. I try to clear it, desperate to keep from bursting into tears in front of everyone. My gaze goes from Dan to Layla to Coach, Mr. Farid, Miss Cheryl, and Hamida. "You didn't have to do any of this."

"What are you talking about?" Miss Cheryl answers. "I'm a starving college student and you just helped me replace my broken laptop. Thank *you*."

"We want to bless you," Mr. Farid says. "Not a single person who gave you any of that would want a cent returned."

Coach hands me the cash from the auction. "You earned this."

My hands close around the money. My throat keeps squeezing. The pain I felt last night has been traded for the joy in this room today. Loss traded for hope.

A severed past for a new community, new songs, a new home.

This is the eleventh trade.

"Thank you," I manage to squeak. "I don't know . . . I . . . thank you."

"Okay, enough sappiness." Dan grins. "Are you going to buy it or what? The shop closes in an hour."

"Yeah, what are you waiting for?" Layla asks. "Get going!"

I look at them all, so full of gratitude and happiness and hope I hardly know what to say. But I know what I have to do. Today is the last day the rebab will be held. And I have the money to get it back.

Coach cups his hands around his mouth. "Go! Go!"

The others take up the chant, their voices filling the gym and echoing from the walls into a song.

I take out my plastic-bag wallet and stuff the rest of the cash into it. "Thank you!" I shout, and then to Dan, "Come on!"

I turn on my heels and run.

29

A LITTLE LESS THAN AN HOUR LATER, DAN AND I
exit the T and take off down the street. We skid around
the corner, and I burst through the door without stopping for breath. The owner's in his usual place, car magazine laid in front of him. He doesn't even glance up
until I reach the counter. Then he frowns.

"I have it," I pant. "I have the money."

The owner shifts in his chair. "Sorry, kid."

My heart falters. "What?"

"You're too late."

A beat passes. I stop breathing, stop existing, for one
long moment.

"W-What?" I repeat.

"Someone bought it on Friday."

"But—but that was last week," I stutter, trying to
make sense of it. "You told me you'd hold it until today."

"She paid more. Plus she traded in that beauty." He nods toward a guitar on the wall. It looks pretty normal to me. "I said from the beginning: I'm not running a charity. She had the better deal."

"That's not fair," Dan growls beside me. "You made a promise."

"Yeah, well." The man shrugs.

I open and shut my mouth. My whole body burns, and I can't find the English words I want to yell at him. But now's not the time for yelling anyway—I need him to work with me. "Where does the new owner live?"

"That's confidential."

I breathe in through my nose, forcing myself to count to five. Dan snorts and wanders away, examining some of the instruments on display near the counter. He's the quick talker—I almost wish he would help me right now, but he also has a temper, so I'm not sorry he's stepped aside.

"Listen, you broke your word—the least you could do is give me a hint. I have to have *that* rebab."

"I can't go giving away personal information. I have the law to uphold."

"You have no honor!" I shout, clenching my hands into fists. "You bought a stolen rebab—how is that upholding the law? And then you went back on your promise!"

"Sure, okay." He closes his magazine. "Go on, kid. I need to close up shop."

My blood sizzles. I want to smash his guitars. I want to throw them through the window.

But Dan reappears at my side and takes hold of my shoulder. "Yes, sir, we'll get out of your hair. Come on, Sami."

He drags me toward the door. When I look back, the shop owner is locking up his cash register, probably rich off his earnings from selling *my* rebab.

"He can't get away with this," I say as soon as the door closes behind us. "There has to be some way to get the information—"

"Already solved it." Dan shows me his cell phone. On the screen there's a picture of the shop ledger, focused on a name—Maliha—and an address. "I had an idea: If she traded in a guitar, she would have recorded her address, just like you did. So I stole a peek at the ledger. And I was right!"

I stare at him. "You are—"

"Brilliant? Gifted?"

"Going to get into serious trouble someday." I grin. "Okay. How do we get to her?"

It takes a minute for us to find the address on Dan's map app. Maliha lives near Boston Medical, which means we're only a thirty-minute bus ride away. We run to catch the next bus. Though it's after rush hour, we still have to squeeze in and stand the whole time. The ride stretches on and on, my head playing through all the ways this could end. We're so, so close to the rebab. So close to everything being right for Eid.

When we arrive at our stop, we wiggle around the other passengers and get dumped on the sidewalk. Dan turns to his map again and leads the way.

We end up going down a quiet street shadowed by trees on both sides. In the early evening, the light turns everything soft and gold tinted. It looks completely different from my part of town, where there's trash everywhere and grit coats the buildings. Here, the redbrick townhouses are placed back from the street, behind bushes and sprouting trees.

"Here's the place—201," Dan says, turning in to a walkway and stepping through a short iron gate.

My pulse beats in my head. I step in front of Dan and press the buzzer. While I wait, I stare at the green-painted door.

It swings open after a few seconds. A young woman wearing a colorful porlaney is in front of me, her scarf covering her hair and lifted to hide her nose and mouth. Her eyes are gray-brown, like my mor's, and I make a connection I should have made in the shop.

Maliha. It's an Afghan name. She's from Afghanistan.

"Assalamu alaikum, khor," I greet her, using the Pashto word for sister. I continue in Pashto, "Tsenga yeh?"

Her eyes widen. In halting English, she asks, "You— Afghan?"

I nod.

She drops her porlaney and grins widely. But I don't notice the grin right away.

Because the skin on her face is melted.

Where it should be normal, it slopes in waxy smears. Like it burned and then froze. Seeing it makes me feel like I have no skin at all, and my first instinct is to back away.

Dan gulps audibly.

I half expect her to lift the porlaney again, but she does not. She does not apologize, either. Her eyes flick to Dan and then to me, the smile still on her misshapen lips.

"It appears I have scared your friend," she says in Pashto. "What is your name?"

"Sami. This is Dan."

"I'm Maliha. Would you both like to come inside?"

I try not to stare directly at her. The rebab is in there. And if her face is scarred, it doesn't matter. Maliha is of my same-language people.

I lift my chin. "Yes, thank you."

30

DAN AND I LEAVE OUR SHOES AT THE DOOR, AND Maliha takes us into a living room. It's decorated like an Afghan house—with real toshaks and a beautiful red Afghan carpet spread across the floor. An older, gray-haired American woman is reading on one of the cushions. She glances up when we enter.

"Ginny, guests," Maliha announces. I hear pride in her voice, though she stumbles through the English. "This—Sami. He is Afghan. And Dan. He is . . ."

"Irish, technically." Dan forces a stiff grin, his face still a bit green. "But American. Bostonian. Yeah."

"Hello! Please make yourselves at home," the woman, Miss Ginny, says, rising. She turns to Dan. "Are you fasting?"

"Um, nope."

Her mouth twitches into a smile. "Well, would you like to come have a cup of tea with me in the other room? Then these two can talk freely in Pashto."

"Oh, yes! That sounds great!" Dan says in a rush. Then he glances at me guiltily. "I mean . . ."

I can't help smiling. "It's fine. Have an extra cup for me."

As they leave, Maliha ushers me to the place of honor at the back of the room. "Ginny is my sponsor," she explains in Pashto. "She hosts a few refugees at a time in her townhouse. She's very kind, and not so bad at brewing chai."

I sit down, but suddenly I can't concentrate on anything Maliha says. Because I see it.

The rebab is resting against the wall.

My baba's rebab, with the beaded tassel from my grandmother, and the mother-of-pearl down its neck.

Maliha notices my gaze. "I found that rebab in Cambridge last week—I could hardly believe my eyes. So rare to come across anything from home!"

The wanting is so strong, I almost can't speak. I have to clear my throat. "I-It is my baba's, actually."

"What?" Maliha asks.

So I recount how the rebab was stolen, and the eleven trades that brought me here. Though it only happened a month ago, it feels as if years have passed, the journey to this apartment has been so difficult. But while I tell Maliha everything that has happened, I find myself smiling at the good times, too.

At the beginning of the month, Baba and I were entirely alone. The loss of the rebab connected me to Dan—first when he found it on eBay, and then when he offered to help after the disastrous trade with Peter. The whole reason I went to the rec center for the first time was because I wanted to see if the iPod could be fixed. And at the rec center I found Layla and Hamida and my team—and Coach, who led me to Mr. Lincoln and Miss Cheryl.

The loss of the rebab also drew me to Mr. Farid and the rest of the community at the mosque. It gathered strangers and mere acquaintances and turned them into friends, brothers, and sisters.

I think of the wad of money in my pocket—scraped and saved and traded and given. It is a strange thing, how the pain has turned to hope. How last night was filled with regret, and today I'm shining with wholeness.

The only piece left is the rebab itself.

After I finish, Maliha exclaims, "What a strange and marvelous story! There must be some magic in the rebab's wood yet."

I nod. I desperately want to offer her the money and take the rebab back. But that is the Western way—over the past month I must have developed an American side, a desire to get what I want as quickly as I can—and instead I sit quietly as she folds her hands on her knees. In Afghanistan, Baba and I couldn't so much as buy a rug without spending hours chatting with the owner. I take a deep breath and feel some of the tension seep away.

"May I tell you how the rebab found me?" Maliha asks, smiling though her eyes look sad. She taps her cheek, where the skin puckers. "It is connected to this."

"How?" I ask, bewildered.

"It begins many years ago. I had an education in Kabul, but when I was fourteen, I had to marry my family's landlord to cover my father's debts. My husband—he was not kind." She rubs her arm, where small circles of shiny scars mark her skin. She lifts her chin. "But I have never been meek. He would not let me attend school, and when he caught me sneaking out, I would be punished. Eventually he kept me locked inside. But when his terrible mother left the home for chai with her friends, I would take his dambora and pluck its strings."

My stomach churns. From her account, I can tell her husband was old-fashioned. In traditional Afghan culture, women are not supposed to play instruments.

She traces her finger along the stretched skin of her jaw. "His mother found me one day and accused me of doing it to attract men." She shakes her head. "I think it was what she and my husband saw as the last of many insults."

"Why did you do it?" I ask, unable to hide a shudder. "Why risk so much?"

"I had no friends, no family, nothing left to me anymore." She shrugs. "I told you I am not meek. The dambora became my voice. Once I had taught myself to play it, I could not stop. It took me to another world—a better one."

I nod. This I understand.

Maliha tilts her head and goes on. "He burned me with acid, and he left. But I am too stubborn to die. I crawled outside the house—he left it unlocked, assuming I was dead—and found my way to a safe place for women. They took me to the hospital. Someone snapped a picture of me before they bandaged the wounds and posted it online. Soon my face was everywhere! Meanwhile, my husband's family was outraged that I had lived and was bringing shame to him. They threatened the shelter. So it was arranged for me to be evacuated, and I came to New York. That was three years past now."

I pause to take all this in. Acid burns are not an unusual form of punishment, but I cannot imagine the sort of person who would do that to someone else. My mor was fortunate—educated, loved by her family, adored by Plar, and doted on by Baba. Was she the exception in our country, or is Maliha? I don't know.

Swallowing, I ask, "What happened then?"

"Well, I lived in another safe home for a long while. I saw many doctors for my body and my mind. I went to English classes, though I am still not good." She laughs a little. "Ginny says I am just impatient. I talk too fast in Pashto for her to understand, but when I speak English, it has more holes than a teapot mender's wares. I do not like to wait for the words to come."

"It isn't an easy language."

"I will conquer it someday." She smiles. "I like to conquer things."

I glance at the rebab. "How did you come to Boston, then?"

"My sponsors think I am ready for the surgery I need, so I have been sent here to have it done at Boston Medical. There are so many refugee centers in Boston—so much help—I may stay instead of returning to New York. I like it here, anyway—I like how green it is on this street." She shifts her legs so that she is kneeling on them. "But most of all I like that you have come today. Ginny is wonderful, and the other Dari and Tajik girls are friendly—they have helped me practice my Farsi—but I had not yet met any Pashtuns in this city. And there is nothing so sad as being homesick right before Eid al-Fitr!"

I nod.

"I thought that God had gifted me with this for Eid," she says, touching the rebab. "I had bought a guitar, but I could not get used to the sound. When I went to sell it, I saw this sitting against the wall behind the counter. You must know, Sami, how it is to feel so alone in such a place. It almost seemed to me that my sweet dambora had been returned, though the two instruments are not very similar."

I nod, a twinge of guilt starting in my stomach. Because I *do* know. And though I want the rebab no less, and though it has to go back to Baba, regret still taints my happiness. If I take it, she won't have this piece of her voice.

But Baba isn't old-fashioned. Not terribly. He would have taught my mor how to play the rebab if she had wanted to learn. He could teach Maliha—I will ask him. I won't take music from her entirely. No one should endure that.

Maliha brushes her fingers across the strings, and they give a soft thrum. Then she lifts the instrument.

"Now I see that God wished this instrument to be a

vessel of his true gift," she says, turning to me and grinning. "For I have met with my brother in a foreign land, and what could bless Eid better than to bless my brother?"

She offers the rebab to me. I stare at it, and then at her.

"No, no," I say, reaching into my pocket. "I have money. I can pay you."

"It is a gift, Sami," she says.

"No, you don't need to, really." I pull out my plastic-bag wallet.

"It is a gift," she insists.

"No, it's too much." I'm shaking my head, and my eyes start to sting again.

Maliha leans over and sets the rebab in my lap. "Now you have refused three times, and I have given three times. You know that I mean it. Do not insult me by protesting more."

I run my hand under the neck of the rebab and wrap my arm around the body, and I know I couldn't argue if I wanted to.

Something for nothing. It isn't a trade, but a gift.

When I glance up at her, she beams. And despite the tears in my eyes, I find myself grinning back.

31

"COME WITH ME TO CELEBRATE IFTAR WITH MY BABA," I blurt suddenly, unsure why I hadn't thought of it before. "He can play this for you—it'll be just like a celebration at home."

"Will there be other women?" she asks, momentarily uncertain.

"Yes—I will invite some!"

"Oh good!" Maliha claps. "Just let me tell Ginny."

She scrambles to her feet and goes into the hall. I take my phone and send texts to everyone I can think of— Layla and her parents, Mr. Lincoln and Miss Cheryl, Hamida, and Coach and Miss Juniper. I don't know how we'll fit them all into our tiny apartment, but I don't care right now. My whole body is light with joy. I can't keep the rebab a secret another day.

I also send a text to Baba. *Coming home soon. Can some friends join us for iftar?*

He answers almost immediately, *Certainly! You know I always make extra in case God brings us guests.*

Maliha pokes her head into the room. "Okay, I'm ready!"

I get up and cradle the rebab in my arms while I follow her out. Dan joins us in the hallway.

He grins when he sees the rebab. "You got it back!"

"Maliha gave it to me." I pull on my sandals by the front door while Dan and Maliha get their shoes. A new thought occurs to me, and I turn to her, bewildered. In Pashto, I ask, "What am I going to do with all the money? I still have eight hundred and ten dollars."

She lifts her eyebrows, pulling on her second sandal. "What do you want to do?"

"Everyone has given so much—I want to give something, too."

"The choice is yours," she says cheerfully, straightening. "There are many refugees like you in this city, and God does love a generous giver."

I nod, decided. I'll have to research programs—perhaps I can talk to Mr. Farid or the imam about places they would recommend. Maybe I could even help Maliha find a dambora! I could get something for Baba, too. Perhaps I could find him some nice lotion to soothe his hands.

There will be time for all that later. Tonight, we celebrate.

And tomorrow, Eid al-Fitr, will be even more joyful.

As we're going out, I say in English to Dan, "We're going to celebrate fast-breaking—iftar—with Baba. I've invited a bunch of the others. Think your mom would be able to join us?"

"I'll ask!" Dan gets out his phone.

"We need to grab some extra snacks on the way there." I pause to grin at Maliha. I'm jittery with happiness. Not only do I have the rebab—I have money to truly host guests. "I think this may be the best Eid ever."

"Alhamdulillah!" Praise be to God. Maliha lifts her porlaney over her nose, but her eyes are squinty with her smile.

Minutes before sunset, I try to shush everyone in the hallway outside my apartment. Mr. Lincoln elbows Coach, and Miss Juniper giggles. Mrs. Michele leans over to play with Jared to calm him down while Mr. Ty shifts his baby carrier. Dan's mom—looking less tired now, with a tilt to her mouth and a mischievous gleam to her eyes—pauses her conversation with Miss Cheryl. Layla, Hamida, and Dan stop poking each other and turn to me. They're holding the grocery bags of snacks we bought on the way.

"I'll go first," I whisper. "Then I'll let you guys in. Okay?"

They nod. Mr. Farid translates into Farsi for Maliha. While he does, I stuff my money back into my pocket. We only spent a little on the food—barely a dent in my earnings. There will be plenty to give.

I take a deep breath and slide my key into the lock. There is no way to hide the rebab—it isn't much smaller than me—so I don't bother putting it behind my back. I tap the door open with my foot and step inside. An Islamic channel crackles over the radio, ready to announce the azaan and fast-breaking. The apartment smells of food and chai and spices.

"Sami jan? Is that you?" Baba calls from the living space. "I'll be just a minute."

"It's me," I say, though my voice trembles slightly. I slip off my shoes and shut the door quietly behind me. "My friends are coming."

"Very good."

My heart has never been so full. I walk to the

doorway and pause. Baba is sitting on one of toshaks, straightening the tablecloth on the floor, but he looks up. Sees me.

Sees the rebab.

For the rest of my life I will remember what this moment feels like.

"Khuday Pak mehriban dey," I whisper. "God is kind."

Confusion and bewilderment flit across his face. I start to laugh, my happiness overflowing. I can't contain it. I offer the rebab to him.

Baba's cracked and worn hands close around the mulberry wood, and he draws the rebab to his lap. He plucks at the strings. A few notes soar into the stillness of our tiny apartment, and I see joy—deep and real—settle in his soul. He looks up at me then, as I open the front door to let in our friends.

Slow and true and wide, he smiles.

AUTHOR'S NOTE

When my sister invited me to visit her in Afghanistan, I said yes.

It was 2011, and I was twenty years old. I spent the months leading up to this trip learning everything I could about a remarkable group of people called the Pashtun, from the way they sit to the way they don't throw away crumbs (they leave them outside for the birds). I focused on the Pashtun because my sister's work was largely conducted in Pashtun regions of the country, and Pashto was her language of study. But Afghanistan is filled with languages and cultures and minority groups, each vibrant with unique forms of hospitality, family life, love, and friendship.

Back then, *The Eleventh Trade* wasn't even a speck in my mind. As I look over this novel, I can see my Afghan friends' fingerprints everywhere. One young man, detained in Greece—long before the migrant crisis appeared in the news—talked about watching from his cell as the Parthenon lit up each night. Another friend, who came to work one day after having been beaten by her own family members, cried with me until I could not tell whose tears were on our hands. During a talk about writing through trauma, another Afghan friend met my eyes and asked, "But how can we look back at trauma without our hearts being broken beyond repair?"

Since 1818, the longest period of peace in Afghanistan has been just forty years, between 1933 and 1973. The unending wars fought on Afghanistan's soil have left wounds that can be seen in the drastic gaps in education between generations and genders, the abject poverty, the bullet holes in mosques, and the scars on survivors. Though foreign peoples such as the Macedonians, Ancient Persians, Mongols, British, Soviets, Pakistanis, and Americans have fought on Afghan soil, journalist Ahmed Rashid said it right when he noted that "no outsider has ever conquered [the Afghans] or claimed their soul."

Afghanistan is immensely beautiful, a land of contradictions. For instance, the hero of Pashtun culture is the warrior-poet, with a rose in one hand and a sword (or AK-47) in the other. Pashtuns adhere to a moral code referred to as Pashtunwali, a set of rules from the times when the tribes of Afghanistan provided the rule of law. The traditions are sometimes inspiring, sometimes severe.

One such tradition describes a way to bring peace between two warring tribes. A dear, white-bearded man told me that a woman from one tribe must bake naan (fresh bread) in her clay oven and carry it to a woman from the other tribe. "When she places the naan into the hands of the other woman, fighting will stop," I was told. "It is in honor of her bravery."

Pashtunwali (and almost every other culture within Afghanistan) also includes strict rules about practical, generous, and self-sacrificial hospitality. The highest honor is to receive a guest—whether the individual is a friend or a stranger, a businessman or a homeless person. Guests are viewed as a gift from God and an opportunity to show God one's respect for humanity by sharing one's resources in order to provide comfort, safety, and refreshment to the guest. Once a visitor is accepted into a Pashtun house, tradition holds that the family must be willing to die before they allow any harm to come to the guest. In Afghanistan, this is not an idle promise.

Throughout *The Eleventh Trade*, it has been a privilege to showcase some of the many complex and remarkable cultural nuances of Sami's homeland to my remarkable readers. A few stylistic choices were made for the sake of readability. First and foremost, the reader should know that the terms "God" and "Allah" could very well be used interchangeably throughout (or the specific Dari or Pashto words could have been used). In this novel, these terms refer to a deity of monotheistic creationism. The words should not be interpreted to have any political significance, although I urge readers to consider the similarities, differences, and common bonds to be found within the languages and cultures encountered in this work.

After my journey, I watched from afar as friend after friend fled Kabul for safer lands. I watched as the period of peace in 2011 slowly slid back into danger.

Then the Taliban attacked my sister.

After hours hiding in a small space, waiting to be found and either killed or rescued, my sister and her friends were saved by Afghan special forces (whom she would like me to thank *very* much!). But even though they survived, those involved in the attack were changed. And in my own small way, I was changed, too. That's what trauma does to you—it draws a mark on the timeline of your life, and the mark stays. I continue to hope there is a way to look back without remaining broken.

A waiter in an Afghan restaurant in Washington, DC, sat down with my sister and made a diagram of the wedding chapter in this book. Together, they took the specifics from the attack my sister had survived and turned them into the scene you read. Attacks such as these are sadly not uncommon.

I read extensively about the migrant crisis during the years of Sami's journey. The southern route into Iran is one of the most dangerous ways out of Afghanistan, where human smugglers frequently lead their clients to their deaths or to years of detention in horrible conditions. In Greece, some refugees were met by a priest who would give them scraps of carpet so they could kneel and pray. Babies were born in ports. As borders close on Afghan refugees, everything becomes more desperate.

Yet even in the darkness of war and upheaval, I have seen in Afghans a beautiful blend of hospitality, honor, and a deep longing for peace. This unyielding hope captured my heart, and I want to spend my life learning it.

Now in the US, I sit in the new homes of recently arrived Afghans, a cup of chai in my hands and a vibrant red rug beneath my bare feet. A teen tells me our run-down, old local library is "*so* beautiful." A child teaches me to play zombie tag. Their mother's eyes light up when I ask her about iftar plans during Ramadan.

As the world turns around us, tilting now and then toward a darker season, we hold that trembling flame of hope in our hands. And we live.

ACKNOWLEDGMENTS

Without community, *The Eleventh Trade* would never have existed.

It all began with Janine Amos at Bath Spa University, who challenged me to write a synopsis for a story completely out of my comfort zone—a story I was never meant to turn into a manuscript.

Whoops?

All of the staff at BSU's fabulous Writing for Young People program: Thank you for pushing and supporting me. Lucy Christopher, Julia Green, and C. J. Skuse in particular—you rock. To my wider class at the MA, particularly Irulan Horner, Jess Butterworth, and Carlyn Attmyn: Thank you for having my back, urging me on, and being a continual blessing. And to all the other folks who poured encouragement into me along the way: the homeschool co-ops (what up, Sonlight!) and my Berry College crew. Chris, Rick, Dr. Meek, Master Greenbaum, and so many others who challenged and mentored me: I'm your biggest fan. Also, of course, a tip of the hat to Dr. Paul at Christopher Newport University—the best of supervisors.

My workshop group: Rebecca Harris, Lindsay Schiro, Emily Morris, Anneka Freeman, and Sarah Driver . . . you're the writing community I always craved but never knew existed. Annie, you Slytherin to my Hufflepuff, master motivator and travel adventurer—I know this probably still needs ~moar emotions~ but don't we all? And my sparkly mermaid goddess of sea-churning, whale-spotting, tea-making fame, Sarah: Any time you want to try fermented shark again, I'll be there to document it— upwind and from a safe distance.

An enormous shout-out to all the experts who made this story make sense: Kaitlyn and Ian (soccer choreography and Man United tips); Erika (middle school teacher extraordinaire); Scott Hetzel and Johnny Geoghegan (combat boot pros); C. and her Afghan coworkers (details on Greek and Afghan instruments); K. (Pashto and Kandahari dialect checks); Richard, Chickie, Adam, and Hannah (Boston specialists); Austin Martin (secondhand stores); Islamic Society of Boston Cultural Center (a wonderfully welcoming mosque); Homayoun Sakhi (Afghan Star and rebab master); the Afghan waiter who wrote out a diagram of the blast scene for my sister; and, of course, Lincoln and Taryn (I hope this fulfills my contract of debt to you; Lincoln—thanks again for the tickets!).

My Third Culture Kids class: You are all remarkable. I want to be you when I grow up.

A special thanks to the Elie Wiesel Foundation for Humanity. Professor Wiesel, when you took my hand after the ceremony, all the force of your love for the world—love that is not blind to its evil—passed into me with a silent commission. Without your kindness, I would never have had the courage to write this story. The world is better—and I am better—because of your courageous hope. May that be your legacy.

Amber and the Skylark Literary team: You took a chance on me, and I'll never forget it. Thank you for always having more faith in me than I have in myself. Kate, Fliss, and all the others who have made this debut a remarkable journey: I couldn't be more pleased to call Roaring Brook and Piccadilly Press my book homes.

Lima, Rasheed, Hamida, Mina, Nizrana—where would this be without you? I am forever humbled by your kindness in reading, your thoughtful feedback, and your unwavering encouragement. *Yak roz didi dost, roze dega didi bradar. Tashakor.*

To my crazy family: Mom (for being my cheerleader in everything), Dad (for logic checks and military input), Jason (for music expertise and general enthusiasm), Laura (for being my biggest critic and staunchest ally), and Philip (for nerd tips and computer advice). And especially Amy. Everything isn't about you, you know. But this kinda is.

Finally, to the master of stories: Christ Jesus. You are kind, even (especially) when I can't see it. Keep breaking my heart with your unbearable, incomprehensible, riotous joy.

Atlanta-Fulton Public Library